GHOST OF A MEMORY

BETH DOLGNER

Ghost of a Memory
Betty Boo, Ghost Hunter Book Three
© 2012 Beth Dolgner

All rights reserved. No portion of this book may be reproduced in any form without permission from the publisher, except as permitted by U.S. copyright law.

ISBN-13: 978-0984915651

Ghost of a Memory is a work of fiction. Names, characters, places, and incidents either are the products of the author's imagination or are used fictitiously. Any resemblance to actual persons, living or dead, businesses, companies, events, or locales is entirely coincidental.

Published by Redglare Press
Book Covers By Melody
Print Formatting by The Madd Formatter

BethDolgner.com

For my dad, Bruce Wyse, who has been a big influence in my journey as a writer.

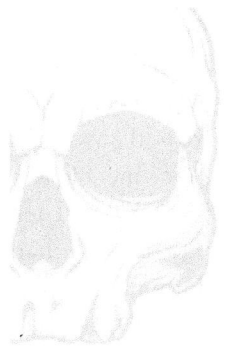

ONE

"I'm pregnant."

There was the briefest moment of utter silence. Even the noise of the restaurant around us seemed to cease as each person at the table processed the words.

Then everyone began talking at once.

"How did this happen?"

"Mother, I think you know how it happens." Daisy's voice was sarcastic, but she was smiling broadly.

"I just meant…I didn't expect…so soon!" Daisy's mom was usually as bubbly and talkative as her daughter, and her sudden loss for words prompted a round of laughter. She covered Daisy's hand with her own. "I'm going to be a grandma. Oh, I'm so happy for you two!"

"Congratulations, Daisy. And to you, Shaun." Daisy's dad Ben was smiling, too, though he looked less overwhelmed than his wife. He playfully nudged her. "I guess you'll have to learn how to change diapers again, Helen."

I was the only one at the table who hadn't responded to the news that my best friend and her husband were going to be parents. My smile, though, said enough for Daisy. "Aunt Betty is going to have to practice, too," she said.

I raised my hands in defense. "No way. I'm not actually family, so I don't have to do diaper duty! I will, however, be more than happy to spoil your child constantly."

"So, how far along are you?" Helen asked.

"About six weeks." Daisy looked at me poignantly. "I didn't even suspect until a few weeks ago, and we wanted to make sure everything was good before we told anyone."

Daisy was looking at me that way for one of two reasons. She was either trying to say, "Sorry I didn't tell you sooner," or she was pointing out the fact that she had put not just her life, but her baby's, at risk for me.

Well, not so much for me as for my ex-boyfriend.

My smile dissolved, and I chewed my lip thoughtfully while I considered all of the implications of Daisy's news. Daisy and Shaun were two of the four members of The Savannah Spirit Seekers, the paranormal investigation team we'd formed while still in college. We'd been investigating reports of hauntings in Savannah, Georgia, for over two years now.

Daisy would probably be able to continue investigating for a while, but I couldn't picture her sitting down on the floor of some old house while seven or eight months pregnant. And even if Daisy could investigate, I realized, some cases might be too dangerous for her now. Shaun, no doubt, would rather be with his wife than hanging out with ghosts. That left me and Lou to investigate, but I hadn't heard from Lou in three weeks.

I suddenly felt very lonely.

I also felt guilty about having put Daisy and Shaun's unborn child at risk when the two of them had agreed to help me rescue my boyfriend Maxwell from his demon captor. Thankfully, no one had gotten hurt on that adventure. In the end, we'd saved Maxwell's life, and then he'd broken up with me.

That had been about a month ago, but I was still nursing those wounds. I sighed, and suddenly Shaun's head was very close to mine. "You okay, Betty?" he asked quietly.

I blinked and cleared my head. "I'm good," I said. "Sorry, it keeps happening." Every time I found something to be happy about, thoughts of losing Maxwell would creep in, and I'd get all melancholy again. Even I was sick of the depressed Betty routine, so I knew all of my friends were, too.

"It's all right," Shaun said.

I pasted my smile back on my face. "So, Daisy, since you're an intuitive woman, can you tell us if it's a girl or a boy?"

Daisy made a show of considering before answering, "Yes."

I managed to keep Maxwell out of my head for the remainder of our dinner. Daisy's parents had come into town for Thanksgiving, which was just a week away. They had always treated me like part of the family since our first meeting during my freshman year of college. Daisy and I had shared a dorm room then, and it was funny to think that now my former roommate was going to be a mom. She and Shaun had been married for a year, and we'd graduated college a short time before their wedding. Life sure could change in a hurry.

When we parted on the sidewalk after dinner, I hugged Daisy. "Congratulations," I said. "I'm really, really happy for you, and you're going to be an incredible mom."

"Thanks. And you're going to be an incredible honorary aunt." Daisy paused. "How are you doing, anyway?"

I shook my head. "This night isn't about me. Besides, I'm fine."

But I wasn't fine. We'd eaten dinner at The Burglar Bar, where I had first met Maxwell. It really wasn't fair that my absolute favorite restaurant in Savannah was also the scene of a memory that was so bittersweet. I had pushed away thoughts of him during dinner, but they crept back into my mind during my short walk home.

Maxwell had broken up with me because it was too dangerous for us to be together. He was a demon, and that meant he'd always live in fear of demon hunters tracking him down. It also meant that other demons might manipulate me, as his friend Tage had done. Tage had wanted me to sell my soul in exchange for Maxwell, whom he had in captivity. We had managed to rescue Maxwell and banish Tage back to hell, but my soul felt pretty weary, even though I hadn't signed it over to anyone.

I had taken it pretty well when Maxwell broke up with me because I understood that he wanted to keep me safe. In the weeks that had followed, though, I'd only gotten more depressed.

I glanced to my left distractedly, checking for oncoming traffic before I crossed the street into one of Savannah's green squares. I had already stepped out into the crosswalk when I stopped and looked sharply in the same direction.

Someone had been standing on the sidewalk about half a block away, his features hidden by the shadows, but I knew immediately that the dark silhouette perfectly matched Maxwell's tall, lean frame. Of course, now that I was really looking, the sidewalk was empty.

I shook my head and continued walking. This made the eighth time in one month that I'd caught a glimpse of Maxwell. Every time, he was hidden in shadows or half-concealed by a crowd of people. And every time I tried to get a closer look, the vision would be gone.

Maybe Maxwell was following me, checking on me even though we weren't dating anymore. It was also possible that I was losing my mind. Someone once told me that ghost hunting and interacting with paranormal entities could make you a little flighty. As I walked, I wondered if I'd bypassed flighty and gone straight to mental.

When I got home, I checked the answering machine out of habit. I wasn't surprised that there were no messages waiting for me. People interested in having The Savannah Spirit Seekers out to investigate a potential haunting were the only ones who ever called that number —well, them and an endless stream of telemarketers—and no one had been calling lately. Things had gotten really busy for The Seekers back in September and October, right after some major publicity for a case we had worked on. But in the past few weeks, we'd gotten only two phone calls.

That was disappointing for me, and not just because I love ghost hunting. It would also have been a welcome distraction now that I was single again.

I slumped down on the couch, and my cat Mina immediately came and curled up by my side. Cats always seem to know when you're feeling bad. I stroked her head with one hand and flipped on the television with the other. It had become my incredibly boring nightly routine.

The next day was Saturday, and it was more of the same empty hours. The only reprieve came when someone knocked on my door around six o'clock in the evening. I recognized my neighbor when I peeked through the window before opening the door. (I'd learned not to open the door to strangers; one knock on the head with a lamp is all it takes to break that habit.)

I live on the bottom floor of an historic carriage house that had been converted into apartments. The mansion that the carriage house is adjacent to is also divided into units. My neighbor had come by to give me a heads up that he was having a party in the courtyard between the two buildings that night. "It might be a little loud," he said, apologizing in advance for any late-night rowdiness.

He didn't even invite me to the party.

I was feeling pretty low by the time Monday morning rolled around, and I was glad to have work to look forward to. Those forty hours a week—more, if I could find an excuse to work late—were the brightest points of my life lately.

I walked into the administration offices of Coastal Health Hospital with a travel mug full of coffee and a barely-balanced plate of cupcakes for the break room. I'd had plenty of time on Sunday to do some baking.

"Oh, Betty, you brought goodies!" our receptionist greeted me. Jeanie deftly reached out and plucked a cupcake off the plate as I teetered past. "Thank you!"

I couldn't help but smile at Jeanie's constant perky demeanor. Her wedding was coming up in a month, and she was even sunnier and more cheerful than usual.

Because Thanksgiving was on Thursday and I also had Friday off, my workweek was only three days long. I was a little disappointed in that, since it also meant a very long and lonely four-day weekend was in store.

I sighed as I sat down at my desk and fired up my computer. "Betty," I told myself out loud, "you have got to get your head on straight. A four-day weekend is supposed to be fun." As if in answer, my eye caught the sticky note I'd put on my computer screen: "Get Awesome Life," it read.

"Okay, I'll try!" I said.

The e-mail that was waiting for me from Daisy wasn't awesome, but it definitely got my day off to an intriguing start.

"Betty! You won't believe what I heard from Mr. Lansford this morning," Daisy's message read. "It's about zombies. Seriously. Call me during lunch."

Daisy had recently gone to work at a prestigious law firm in Savannah. Mr. Lansford, the head of the firm, came from Old Savannah stock, and he was a prominent member of the community. Daisy had gotten the job through Mr. Lansford's son Carter. It was all a little strange because, until recently, neither Daisy nor I had liked Carter. Lately, though, he had been nicer than usual, and he had really come through for us by teaming up on a couple of paranormal investigations with The Seekers. He had also gone with me to save Maxwell, and that right there had earned Carter a free pass for any of his usual snobbery.

Carter talking about zombies was one thing—it wouldn't be the first time—but Mr. Lansford broaching the subject was definitely mysterious. I'm just a marketing assistant at Coastal Health, so I can't get away with making personal calls on company time. Lunch suddenly couldn't come soon enough.

Eventually, after wading through a stack of work that had to be done before Thanksgiving, the clock on my computer read noon. I wasted no time in closing the door to my tiny office and dialing Daisy on my cell.

"Oh, my gosh, Boo!" she answered. "Carter is totally up to something."

"Of course he is."

"But he's up to even more than usual. Mr. Lansford said that Carter is going to be part of some big investigation on an island off the coast, and apparently, he's investigating zombies instead of ghosts."

"First of all," I said, "there's no such thing as zombies. I don't care what Carter claims. And second, if there's something ridiculous going on in the paranormal community, then of course Carter is involved in it."

"Even Carter's dad is excited about this one. There's

some historic preservation group involved, and supposedly it's a really big deal."

"Daisy, are you actually defending Carter Lansford?"

"No. Well, yes. I mean, he did get me the job here at his dad's firm. And I know you don't believe Carter's hype, but Mr. Lansford is a down-to-earth guy who wouldn't go around talking about zombies for no good reason."

I laughed. "As long as Carter doesn't get bitten and turn into a zombie, too. He'd never be happy without his regular manicures."

Daisy didn't hang up until promising me twice that she'd ply Mr. Lansford for more details.

I spent the rest of my afternoon trying to picture Carter's pretty-boy looks transformed into the rotting flesh of a zombie. I giggled more than once.

Before I left work on Wednesday, Jeanie invited me to the bar in the basement of the Pink House for pre-Thanksgiving drinks. She and her fiancé were meeting a few friends there, and since the Pink House is walking distance from my apartment, she wouldn't take any excuse for me not to be there.

"Besides," Jeanie added as I walked out the door at five, "one of the guys coming tonight is really cute and really single."

I groaned loudly, hoping she would get the hint that I didn't want to be set up with anyone. Not right now, at least.

Unfortunately, Jeanie did not get the hint. I showed up in blue jeans and a light green sweater—it looked good with my auburn hair—and was surprised to see that Jeanie was wearing a black cocktail dress.

"Wow, I feel underdressed," I said in greeting. "You look gorgeous."

Jeanie tapped me on the shoulder playfully. "Oh, stop. Greg and I had dinner upstairs, so we decided to dress," she said. I had met Greg a few times, when he'd stopped by Coastal Health, but tonight Jeanie's fiancé looked like a model from a men's clothing catalog. He wore a wide smile, just like Jeanie.

I guessed that Jeanie had ordered a cocktail or two while she and Greg ate in the nice restaurant upstairs, on the main floor of the Pink House. I'd only eaten there once, but the basement bar was a great place to go on a date. It was dark and cozy, with a blazing fireplace on each end and an old woman singing and playing on a piano. I thought it was probably what bars were like decades ago, when people got dressed up to go have a drink. I would have asked Maxwell, but he and I had never made it there together.

No sooner had I greeted Jeanie and Greg, and gotten an immediate sense of her high level of tipsy, than she grabbed me by the waist and pushed me in the direction of a cluster of people sitting on the couch and chairs by one of the fireplaces. "Everybody, this is Betty Boorman. She's the ghost hunter I was telling you about!"

I got a few polite hellos before Jeanie steered me toward one particular guy. "This is Dennis. Dennis, Betty. Here, Betty, sit."

Dennis flashed a smile at me. I tried to smile back, but I'm pretty sure that all I managed to do was look awkward. "Hi," I said.

"Nice to meet you. Can I get you a drink?" Before I could answer, Dennis had flagged down a waitress. I ordered a glass of cabernet, then sat back and took a long look at the man who was currently giving me A Brief History of Dennis. He was a little heavyset, but he had nice features and dark, exotic eyes. Dennis clearly had no lack of self-confidence. My drink had already been delivered to me, and I was three or four sips in before he finally stopped talking. "So," he said, "what about you?"

I made pleasant conversation as much as I could, but I could tell that Jeanie had given Dennis some sort of "she's single and needs a man" speech earlier in the evening. I didn't want to be rude, but I was so not interested.

I bought our second round—no way was I going to let him buy all my drinks—then made a show of yawning. "I'm so tired," I said. "Two glasses of wine is just putting me to sleep. I think I'd better head home."

I stood and extended my hand. "It was really nice to meet you," I said, but even as I spoke, Dennis stood and shook his head.

"I'll walk you to your car," he said.

"I actually walked here from home. Thank you, though."

"That's right, Jeanie said you were close. How about I walk you home? It's awfully late for you to be wandering the streets."

I wanted to tell Dennis that being out at all hours of the night was pretty normal for me, but instead I opted for a polite, "No, thanks."

He didn't take the hint. He and Jeanie had that in common.

Jeanie saw us to the door, hugging both of us and giving me all kinds of significant looks.

Dennis kept up a constant stream of chatter on the way home, telling me something about how he had played football in college and had been some kind of star player. I wasn't really listening because I was pretty sure we were being followed.

I had first noticed something odd when we walked up the stairs and onto the sidewalk in front of the Pink House.

My eyes had turned to the square across the street, and I saw someone standing there underneath an oak tree. That someone had clearly been facing our direction. I instantly thought of Maxwell, but, as usual, when I tried to focus, the image just dissolved into the shadows.

I wrote this one off as an overactive imagination, but two blocks later, a glance down an alley showed the same form, staring out from the first level of a fire escape. I actually stopped that time, but the fire escape was empty when I squinted and peered into the alley.

We were just a block from my apartment when I began to hear footsteps behind us. They were quiet but deliberate, moving a little faster than the quick pace I was keeping in hopes of getting rid of Dennis as soon as possible. I tried to glance behind me casually, but saw nothing, so I stopped and turned around to see who was behind us.

There was no one.

Dennis had just given me a confused look when I'd stopped at the mouth of the alley, but this time he said, "What are you looking at?"

I shrugged. "Nothing."

He laughed. "What, is there a ghost following us or something?" I detected a note of condescension in his voice. Despite Jeanie having introduced me as a ghost hunter, Dennis had never once asked me about it. When I mentioned it during our conversation at the Pink House, he had quickly changed the subject to something about himself.

I ignored his question and continued walking. I really needed to stop seeing Maxwell everywhere I went. No, I corrected myself, I need to stop *thinking* I'm seeing Maxwell everywhere. I couldn't even walk home in peace.

Maybe, I suddenly thought, that's the point. Maxwell's job as a demon is to spread chaos and fear. The more he disrupted someone's life, the happier he was. I hadn't experienced that side of Maxwell. It was his true nature, I knew, but he'd always treated me well because he loved me. Still, I'd heard some of his stories about tormenting other people. He drove one woman to suicide after he kept her from saying good-bye to her dying husband.

Now that we weren't dating anymore, maybe Maxwell had decided that I should be his next victim.

That thought filled me with fear. I was far too familiar with the power of demons, and I knew that protecting myself from one took a lot of strength, a lot of faith, and a really sharp blessed knife.

Maybe I should start carrying a blessed knife, I thought. Just a small one that I could hide in my purse.

It's probably a good thing that I didn't have a knife in my purse, though, because I probably would have used it in the next instant when a burly man wearing a stained tee-shirt and ripped jeans suddenly stepped in front of me.

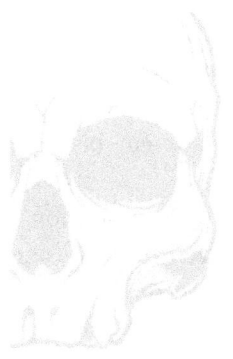

TWO

I stopped abruptly to avoid walking face-first into the man's chest. He had close-cropped blonde hair, and the scowl on his weathered face looked permanent. Dennis stopped, too, and I felt his tense arm wrap around my shoulders.

"Do you ever feel like you're being followed?" the man said to me.

"Have you been following me?" I hadn't intended to answer his question with a question, but of the two of us, I felt like he was the one who should be explaining things.

"I saw you come out of the Pink House, but then I cut over here on another street. It wasn't me following you."

I narrowed my eyes. "Are you saying someone else was following me?"

The man nodded grimly.

Great. Here I'd been trying to convince myself that it was all in my head, and this guy was confirming that someone had been shadowing me.

Dennis had been listening to our conversation, his head turning from me to the man like he was watching a tennis match. Finally, he said, "Are you threatening us?" His arm slid from my shoulders, and he stepped toward the man, his chest bowing out.

"I'm not, and you need to back away. I'm not going to

hurt you or your girlfriend." At that, the man paused and gave me a curious look. "So it really is over between you, then. I don't think he's taking it well."

I put my face in my hands for a moment before I looked back up at him. "You're a hunter."

"I'll be able to retire if I can accomplish my mission." The man glanced at Dennis, and I realized he was using vague terms to keep Dennis from catching on. I guess it would be pretty hard to introduce yourself as a demon hunter. I didn't know what the bounty on Maxwell was, but I did know that it must be a significant chunk of cash.

"He's not my boyfriend," I said, pointing at Dennis. "Besides, if you know it's over between me and Maxwell, then why are you following me? It won't get you anywhere."

The hunter laughed. "Of course it will. Don't you know he's been following you? Not all the time, but enough that I'll be able to catch up with him if I keep tabs on you."

So I wasn't delusional after all. I really was catching glimpses of Maxwell everywhere I went. I wasn't sure if that made me feel better or if it made me worry more. If Maxwell was following me, then it was either because he still loved me or because he wanted to torment me. And if it was the former, then that had stalker written all over it, and I failed to see the romance in it.

I considered telling the hunter to stop tailing me, but I knew it wouldn't make any difference to him. He considered himself on a mission from God, and if that meant shadowing me in order to reach Maxwell, then he'd do it whether I liked it or not.

"Please don't harm me or any of my friends," I said firmly. "I'm not dating Maxwell anymore, and I have no contact with him." With that, I took Dennis by the arm and made a wide circle around the hunter. He didn't try to stop me.

"What the hell was that about?" Dennis asked as soon as the hunter was behind us. He was throwing angry glances over his shoulder, and I tightened my grip on his arm in case he was thinking of going back to pick a fight.

"It's a long story. My ex-boyfriend has a bad history, and he's got some people after him. I guess that guy didn't get the message that we'd broken up."

"That dude made it sound like your ex was stalking you."

"Well, I haven't seen him, so if he is, then he's being really sneaky about it."

We finally reached my apartment, and Dennis made a hasty farewell, shaking my hand and mumbling a quick, "Nice meeting you." At least the encounter with the hunter had changed Dennis's mind about trying anything romantic.

I shut my door and locked it, then leaned my forehead against the cool wood. I had thought that I was done with demon hunters forever. The last thing I wanted was some hunter wandering around after me. I wasn't sure if I was more upset about the idea of being tailed or the constant reminder of Maxwell.

The hunter's words came back to me suddenly. He'd said that Maxwell wasn't taking our breakup well, and I wondered if Maxwell was as upset about the end of our relationship as I was. After being in human form for hundreds of years, I was sure that he'd gotten used to moving on. Or maybe he hadn't. As mean as it sounded, I was a little comforted by that idea.

I also knew that, whatever Maxwell's reason was for popping up everywhere I went, I had to warn him. I still loved him and would still do whatever I could to keep him safe from demon hunters.

Calling Maxwell would be the easiest thing to do, but I was hesitant to talk to him. I sighed. "Let's just get it over with," I said out loud.

I pulled out my cell phone and called Maxwell before I could wimp out. I still had his number (area code "666," of course) programmed in my phone.

But, after one ring, I got a recording that the number was no longer in service.

Had Maxwell changed his number just so I couldn't call him? Surely not. I hadn't called him at all after our breakup, so if he had changed his number, then it wasn't because of me.

That left me with an even less attractive option: going to Maxwell's house to warn him in person. I didn't like that idea, though, and not just because I wasn't ready to see him again. I worried that showing up on Maxwell's doorstep would send a blatant message to the hunter, one that could have negative repercussions for me. So far, the hunters had steered clear of harming me, but if I warned Maxwell out in the open like that, then they would know whose side I was on.

And I did not want to have my name added to a demon hunter's list.

I realized with some surprise that I was still standing at my front door. I plopped down on the couch and picked up the TV remote, but it sat unused in my hands. How could I get a message to Maxwell without being caught by the hunters?

If I could just give him a note, or say something when I caught a glimpse of him in the shadows, then maybe I could pass along a warning.

A note seemed like my best bet, but there was still a chance that it would be intercepted. Unless, I realized, I left the note in a place where the demon hunters didn't go.

"Lieutenant Griffin," I called.

My Spirit Sentry answered immediately, banging the blinds in my dining room once.

"Has Maxwell been showing up here when I'm not home?"

Usually my ghost gave one bang on the blinds for yes and two bangs for no. I took his silence as a show of stubbornness.

"I know you really like Maxwell," I said. "Believe it or not, I still really like him, too. I need to get a warning to him, and if he comes here at all, leaving a note would be the easiest way."

Still, there was obstinate silence from Lieutenant Griffin. The lieutenant had been a soldier in the Civil War, but he was killed out at Fort Pulaski when the Union Army attacked. His spirit had wandered the old fort until Maxwell had found him and brought him to my apartment for a new kind of guard duty. I had often suspected that Ambrose Griffin was more loyal to Maxwell than he was to me.

"Please, Lieutenant," I tried again. "There is a demon hunter who's getting too close to Maxwell, and I need to warn him. Has he been here?"

This time, there was one quiet bang.

"A lot?"

Lieutenant Griffin didn't answer, and I took that as a yes. It was a frightening thought. If Maxwell was coming to my apartment when I wasn't home, then maybe he was coming when I was asleep, too. I was a heavy sleeper and would probably never know. I considered asking Lieutenant Griffin about it, then decided I was happier not knowing. Instead I asked, "Do you think he'll come here again soon?"

This time, the blinds banged firmly.

I thanked my ghost for his help, as much as his affirmative answers bothered me. At least I'd be able to warn

Maxwell. I wrote him a note and left it on my dining room table. Then I wrote three more. I taped one to the screen of my TV, one went on my dining room blinds, and the third I managed to attach to the cord from my ceiling fan. Hopefully, Maxwell would see one of them.

I kept the note short and simple. I didn't want to drag any emotion into this, but I made it very, very clear that he needed to keep his distance.

I woke up early on Thursday, even though it was a holiday. My mom was expecting me at her house on the Southside by eleven so I could help fix Thanksgiving dinner for the aunt, uncle, three cousins, and one neighbor who were all coming over. I had never felt so unenthusiastic about Thanksgiving in my entire life.

There was no way I was going to fall back asleep, so I dragged myself out of bed and headed for the coffee maker. I wasn't paying attention and walked face-first into the note hanging from my ceiling fan.

I took my time drinking my coffee and finally left my apartment at ten with a reminder to Lieutenant Griffin to be on the alert for Maxwell. "If he shows up, you bang those blinds until he sees the note," I told him.

There was little traffic on the short drive to Mom's, and she was still in her dressing gown when she opened the door. The smell of pumpkin pie wafted onto the front porch. She had probably been up for hours already, too busy cooking to even get dressed.

I opened my mouth to make a joke about her appearance, but Mom's drawn face stopped me.

"Oh, honey," she said. "We need to talk."

I was instantly alert. "What's wrong?" I asked. I

thought maybe something had happened to a relative. Maybe cranky old great-uncle Elijah had finally died.

Mom just shook her head sadly. "Nothing's wrong with me. It's you, Betty. He told me everything."

A vision of Maxwell ringing my mom's front doorbell suddenly flashed in my mind. Had he come to her house just to warn her how depressed I'd been lately? Or, worse, had he come over in an effort to sow discord in my life?

Mom ignored my repeated question of "Who?" Instead, she just took me by the hand and led me inside. She went straight to the stiff couch in the formal living room, a sure sign that we were about to have a serious talk.

The last time she'd sat me down there was to warn me about the perils of promiscuity at college. There had never, ever been a conversation on that couch that wasn't really awkward.

"Mom, who told you about me? Did Maxwell come here?"

"That guy you dated? Of course not. I would never allow that demon into my home."

I tried to form a sentence several times, but every word I tried to speak came out garbled. Mom looked at me keenly, and I suddenly felt really self-conscious. I sat back and looked down at my lap to avoid her gaze. "Lou must have told you," I finally said. He was the only one of my friends who might go to my mother with that kind of information. I knew that Daisy and Shaun would never share my secret.

"Yes. He's a very good friend to you, Betty."

"I just can't believe he told you about Maxwell."

"What do you mean? We barely talked about Maxwell at all."

I looked up and saw the confusion on Mom's face. "But you said he was a demon."

Mom sat up straight. "Of course I did! The way he just

disappeared on you was abominable. I'm surprised more of your friends aren't calling him mean things."

A short laugh escaped my lips, but Mom's next comment sobered me quickly. "Why, did he do something else I should know about?"

"No, Mom. He was a great boyfriend." When I had thought Maxwell had been banished to hell by a hunter, I'd told her that Maxwell had suddenly stopped calling me and that I couldn't get in touch with him. My heartbreak wasn't feigned, even though the reason I gave her for it was a lie. She didn't know Maxwell was a demon, so I'd never told her about the aftermath of his encounter with the hunter.

I felt vastly relieved that Mom was still in the dark about Maxwell, but I was also concerned about what Lou might have told her. I asked her for all the details.

"He told me how upset you've been since Maxwell fell off the face of the earth," Mom said. "Lou is concerned that you're still so affected by all of this, and he thinks you might need help getting over Maxwell."

I stood, my hands on my hips. "Lou wouldn't know because he's not speaking to me anymore. I haven't heard from him in weeks."

"Goodness, why not? I thought he was one of your closest friends. He's one of The Seekers with you!"

I sat back down on the couch. "He was a close friend. He didn't like Maxwell, but now that we've broken up, I don't understand why Lou won't speak to me."

Lou Miles was the fourth member of The Savannah Spirit Seekers, and he was our tech guy who always went over the hours of video and audio recordings we got during investigations. He had been a great friend to me, even helping me rescue Maxwell. I knew that had been a sacrifice for Lou because he was studying to become a demon hunter. No, I corrected myself, he already was a demon hunter. He'd banished Maxwell's captor Tage like a pro. I knew it had been a real moral dilemma for Lou, banishing one demon to save the other.

After that, Lou had simply disappeared from my life. He knew that Maxwell and I had broken up—Daisy had seen to it personally that Lou got the news—but it hadn't made a difference. I missed him.

Mom patted my knee. "I'm sorry, honey. I can see the difference in you, too, you know. Even over the phone, you sound so dejected. I think you need a change of scenery. A vacation."

I wrinkled my nose at the idea, but it had merit. If I got away from Savannah for a few days, then maybe it would keep Maxwell—and any demon hunters who were after him—away from me.

I insisted that Mom go take a shower and get dressed while I took over basting the turkey and preparing some of the side dishes. By the time Mom re-emerged in the kitchen, the rest of our guests had arrived. The house was full of noise, and my youngest cousin kept tugging on the hem of my shirt to ask if dinner was ready yet.

It was actually a nice distraction, and I didn't think of Maxwell again until we were all sitting down to eat. Mom's dining room table wasn't that big, and we were squeezed in elbow-to-elbow. Before everyone filled their plates, my uncle asked, "What's everyone thankful for this year? We'll start with you, Edna."

Mom smiled and looked at me. "I'm thankful that I have a daughter who's turned into such a wonderful young woman."

"Thanks, Mom," I said quietly. My aunt picked up the thread, and then it was my turn. I sat and thought for a moment. I had no boyfriend, The Seekers were virtually inactive at the moment, and I was feeling lonelier than I ever had in my life. What did I have to be thankful for? I looked around the table. I did have loving relatives, and I felt like Daisy and Shaun were an extension of that family. I grinned suddenly as the answer presented itself. "I'm thankful that I'm going to be an honorary aunt," I said. I filled everyone in on Daisy's news. Everyone, especially Mom, expressed a lot of enthusiasm.

Thanksgiving dinner turned out to be more enjoyable than I had anticipated. I realized I had been focusing too much on the gaps in my life instead of looking at the good things I had.

The feeling didn't last long. On my way home that afternoon, I called Lou. I didn't even plan to confront him about going to my mom to talk about me. I just wanted to wish him a Happy Thanksgiving. Instead, my call went to voicemail. I left a message, asking him to please call me.

I waited the rest of the day. Lou never called.

When my cell phone rang on Friday morning, I jumped to grab it from its spot on the dining room table, sure it was Lou calling. It wasn't. Instead, I saw Carter's name on the screen.

Oh, this was going to be good.

"Betty, good morning!" Carter had never addressed me so enthusiastically, and I was instantly on alert.

"You're up to something," I said.

"Damn right I am. And it has to do with you."

"Does it have to do with zombies, too? I hear you're hanging out with the living dead these days."

Carter's tone was deflated when he answered me. "Who told you?"

"Daisy. Apparently your dad has been bragging about you."

"Because this is a big deal for me. It can be for you, too. Can you meet me at The Big Bean Theory later?"

I agreed to meet Carter at the coffee shop at one. There was no way I could resist hearing Carter spout off about zombies. Seriously, could he get any more ridiculous?

I checked myself. Carter had been steadily improving in the past month or so. In fact, I was beginning to consider him a friend, which meant we had made great progress in our relationship. Carter was a spoiled Southern rich boy, and he was used to getting what he wanted, which meant that it hadn't gone over well when I'd turned him down for a date a few years before. Since then, we'd become rival ghost hunters, The Savannah Spirit Seekers versus East Coast Paranormal Authorities.

Over the past few months, though, we'd had to work together on some cases. Our usual animosity had begun to dwindle, and these days we were downright nice to each other.

I kept that in mind while I walked to The Big Bean Theory. Carter had listened to me talk about Maxwell with an open mind, and I needed to do the same for him, even if the subject was zombies.

Carter was already there when I walked in. He was sitting at a table in the front window, looking out over Barnard Street. He was wearing khaki slacks and a striped dress shirt. Combined with his perfectly-coiffured blonde hair, Carter looked like the stereotypical preppy from a college movie.

Carter greeted me with as much enthusiasm as he'd shown on the phone. It was a little disconcerting. "You will be so excited when I tell you my news!" he said.

I put up a hand to stop him from launching into his story. "If we're about to have a serious conversation about zombies, then I need caffeine first."

When I was sitting across from Carter with a steaming mocha latte in front of me, I motioned to him to begin.

"There's an island off the coast that is suffering from a zombie infestation."

"You've lost me already," I said. "Zombies, Carter? Really?"

Carter huffed out a breath. "You're the one who dated a demon, and you don't believe me about zombies? Come on, Betty."

I nodded. "You're right. I promised myself I'd keep an open mind about this. Sorry. Go ahead."

"Thank you. As I was saying, it's an island south of here, off the coast of Darien. There used to be a really fancy resort there, but the place went under years ago. Now, an historic preservation team wants to bring the resort back to life. They're planning to turn the island into a wildlife refuge, and they want to restore the old buildings and open the place up to tourists.

"The guy leading the team called me a couple of weeks ago. He says they went to the island and ran into a couple of zombies, just roaming around."

"Stop right there," I interrupted. "First, how does a zombie wind up on some island? And second, how did this guy even come to the conclusion that the people he saw were zombies? Maybe they were just," I waved my hand, "people who live out there."

"It's an uninhabited island," Carter assured me. "That team has been all over the island numerous times to conduct their research into this project, and this is the first time they've come across anyone. Also, the people they saw weren't ordinary people. They were clearly dead."

"But they were wandering around?"

"Yes. There are a few characteristics that all zombies have." Carter began ticking off points on his fingers. "Their movements are awkward and slow, their flesh is rotting, they are unable to speak, and they need no food or water. Since I have experience with zombies, the preservation team asked me to come investigate."

I remembered Carter once mentioning that he'd dealt

with zombies in Mexico. I had laughed it off at the time, but Carter looked perfectly serious right now. He clearly believed everything he was saying.

"If your team is doing the investigation, then why did you want to talk to me?" I asked.

Carter shrugged. "Ron and Kerri said they can't take the time off work, but I think they're really just wimping out. They haven't been the same since Kerri got hurt by that demon at Sam MacIntosh's house."

Carter paused and hesitated before he spoke again. "Plus, I need somebody with me that I can trust not to panic."

"What do you mean?"

"Zombies aren't easy to deal with. I can't show up with someone who's going to run screaming the first time they see one. You've faced demons, so I think you can handle zombies. I'm planning to spend two weeks on the island, and I'm leaving the week after next. Do you want to go with me?"

Two weeks was a serious commitment to one investigation. I had to admit, though, I was intrigued by Carter's story. Even if the supposed zombies turned out to be something completely normal (I still refused to believe that zombies actually existed), it might be fun to check out the place, anyway. I had built up enough vacation time at work and had no other plans for it. Plus, Mom had suggested that maybe I needed to get away for a while so I could separate myself from reminders of Maxwell.

Maxwell. If I didn't announce where I was going, then Maxwell wouldn't be able to follow me. More importantly, that demon hunter wouldn't be able to follow me. I could help keep Maxwell safe by disappearing for two weeks.

"Okay, Carter," I said. "I'm in."

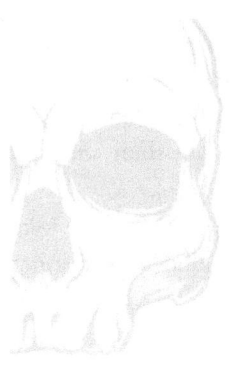

THREE

The first thing I did when I got home from the coffee shop was ask Lieutenant Griffin if Maxwell had materialized in my apartment while I'd been gone. I got two bangs on my blinds in answer. It was the same answer I'd received when I'd gotten home from Thanksgiving dinner the day before.

"For once I want to be followed, and I'm not," I said, shaking my head.

I left my apartment several more times that weekend, and every time I got home, I asked Lieutenant Griffin the same question. The answer was always negative.

When I got to work on Monday, I immediately put in my vacation request for the next two weeks. It was last-minute notice, and I hoped my boss would approve it without giving me a hard time.

I should have known better. My boss came into my office exactly three minutes after I'd e-mailed my request form to the human resources director. "May I ask where you're planning to go?" he asked, his tone primed for a lecture.

I hesitated. My boss was not a fan of my ghost hunting, so I knew that admitting why I was leaving town would not go over well. At the same time, I didn't want to lie to him. "A friend of mine has connections with an historic preservation group," I finally said. "I've got an opportunity to volunteer with them at an old resort that's undergoing renovation."

Most Savannah residents are fans of historic preservation. The revitalized downtown, with buildings from as far back as the 1700s, draws thousands of tourists every year. I knew that I was using the angle that was most likely to gain approval in my boss's eyes.

Luckily, my instinct had been right. He gave his hearty approval and told me to come back with lots of pictures.

Carter was leaving for the island on Friday, and he had agreed to wait until I got off work so that I could ride with him. That meant I had to be packed and ready to go by the time I left for the office Friday morning, so I didn't have a lot of time to prepare.

I did all of my laundry on Monday night because I was planning to have dinner at Daisy and Shaun's on Tuesday. Daisy had already agreed to take care of my cat Mina while I was gone, but I wanted to see her and Shaun before I left town.

They were both as mystified as me by Carter's claims about zombies. "If I wasn't pregnant, I'd be right there with you," Daisy said over our baked ziti. "Just to see Carter's disappointment when he realizes the stories are bunk."

I shrugged. "Maybe there's some truth to the claims. The preservation team might have seen apparitions that looked like rotting corpses."

Daisy narrowed her eyes at me. "Watch out for Carter. I'm not sure I like the idea of you two taking off to a deserted island together."

"What, do you think he's going to stab me or something?"

Shaun laughed. "She's worried about the opposite."

"That I'll stab Carter?"

"No, that you two will get along too well," Shaun

corrected. "Daisy owes her job to Carter, but she's afraid you'll start to like him a little too much."

Daisy nodded, but unlike Shaun, she saw no humor in the scenario. "He's been really nice to you, Betty. You even went to that Halloween party with him. You're both ghost hunters, you're both intelligent people, you're close to the same age. In theory, he's a great match for you."

"In reality, though, he's stuck-up and annoying. Daze, you have nothing to worry about." Now I was laughing, too. "Besides, shouldn't you be more worried about me facing zombies?"

Daisy shook her head seriously. "No, I'd rather stare down a zombie than see you all googly-eyed about Carter."

I didn't get out the door after dinner until I'd promised no less than five times not to get involved with Carter. I rolled my eyes as Daisy implored me to shun any advances Carter might make. It wasn't so much her persistence that frustrated me, but the fact that she wasn't the first to assume there might be something between Carter and me. Even Maxwell had once flirted with the idea, although, to his credit, he was starving and locked inside a wooden crate at the time. He had a valid excuse for thinking crazy thoughts, but not Daisy. I felt almost offended that anyone, let alone my best friend, would suspect me of falling for Carter.

Ew.

With those kinds of thoughts, I was immediately suspicious when my phone rang late Thursday night. I answered it to hear Carter say, "Make sure you bring something nice to wear."

"Nice like a cocktail dress?" I asked.

"Nice like jeans that aren't ripped up, and maybe some nice tops instead of your usual tee-shirts."

"We're going to be on an uninhabited island. Who's going to see me?"

"We want to impress these people," Carter said.

I suddenly realized that I hadn't asked him the most important question regarding the investigation. "Where are we sleeping, anyway? Are we going to be in tents?"

"Certainly not. Part of the old resort is still in good enough shape that we can stay in it. It won't be fancy, but it's better than a tent."

I frowned and idly said, "We're living in the ruins of an old resort, but you want me dressed nice. That makes zero sense, Carter."

"Just do it for me," he growled.

"Fine, fine. Any other requests? I can wear some pretty jewelry or maybe a nice pair of heels."

Carter sighed impatiently. "I'm already second-guessing my decision to invite you, but I'll pick you up at 5:30 tomorrow." With that, he hung up, leaving me to wonder about his bizarre request.

Despite Carter getting on my nerves on the phone the night before, I was really excited about the investigation when I got home from work on Friday. I felt better than I had in weeks.

I felt even better when I realized that the note hanging from the chain on my ceiling fan was missing. I looked for it on the floor, but it wasn't there. "Maxwell came by today, didn't he?" I asked.

Lieutenant Griffin gave an affirmative bang.

I wasn't sure why Maxwell had taken the entire note. If he'd wanted to let me know he'd received the message, then he could have just written a response to me. Either way, I was glad that I'd done my part in warning him. Now it was up to Maxwell to take my advice and stop tailing me.

Thankfully I'd done my final bit of packing in the

morning before work because I got home with just ten minutes to spare. Carter knocked on my door right at 5:30. I scratched Mina behind the ears and told both her and Lieutenant Griffin that I'd be back in two weeks. I also reminded the lieutenant not to be surprised when Daisy popped over to feed Mina. The last thing I needed was him thinking she was an intruder.

Carter led the way while I carried my own luggage out to his Mercedes. Such a gentleman.

It took us about forty-five minutes to reach Darien, which is a straight shot south on the interstate. Carter and I made some small talk on the way, but he was unusually quiet and introspective. Whenever I pried him for more details of the investigation, he would only give me vague answers.

The last rays of the sun had disappeared by the time we got off the interstate and wound east along a two-lane road that paralleled a river. We pulled into the parking lot of what looked like a factory, and as soon as we got out of the car, I recognized the sharp smell of a paper plant. "What are we doing here?" I asked. I was pinching my nose, so I sounded like I had both a bad cold and lungs full of helium.

"Parking," was Carter's short answer.

"Do you mean that you're leaving your precious Mercedes all alone here for two weeks?"

Carter shrugged as if it were no big deal, but as he opened the trunk I heard him mumble, "I should have hired a driver to bring us down."

We were alone in the parking lot, and there wasn't another building in sight. It was a lonely spot, so I was surprised when two men emerged from the surrounding darkness. I jumped and let out a quiet yelp, but Carter was unaffected.

"Carter, welcome," one of the men said. He was tall

and fit, and he moved with the stride of an athlete. His tanned face was topped by dark blonde hair. When he got closer, he turned his attention to me, and I could see his green eyes. They looked faded, like he'd spent years out in the sun, but they had a quickness to them. This guy doesn't miss anything, I thought. "You must be Betty Boorman," he said, extending a hand. "I'm Joseph Stryker with the National Trust for Historic Preservation. It's so good to meet you."

"Thank you for inviting me to come along," I said. Joseph's grip was strong, and he looked me in the eyes while we shook hands. Something about his gaze gave me a little bit of a thrill.

Joseph's companion was short and chubby, and he had a shiny bald spot in the middle of his brown hair. He wore wire-rim glasses and looked like he would have been more at home in an office. "I'm Rob Sanders. A pleasure."

Rob's handshake was limp and slightly sweaty. It fit his demeanor perfectly.

As we stood there, a white van pulled up and parked next to us. The driver and his passenger got out, called a precursory hello, and immediately began to unload bags and big plastic bins from their van.

"I'll help you haul those to the boat," Joseph offered.

I gave Carter a sidelong glance. "Boat?" I said quietly.

"Of course. How else would we get to the island?"

"I guess I had pictured a bridge in this scenario." But, of course, if the island was deserted, then that meant it wasn't attached to civilization in any way. I suddenly realized just how very disconnected I was going to be from everything that was familiar to me. It was disconcerting to think that for the next two weeks of my life, the only thing I had to remind me of home was Carter.

I followed the five men across the street, where a boat sat at a small dock. The river, I realized, must feed out into the ocean, where our mysterious island was. I hauled my suitcase along, but once we were on the dock, Joseph took it and swung it onto the boat with one hand. He reached his other hand to me as I climbed on board. The deck of the small boat was littered with old fishing lures and bait buckets, and there was no interior cabin. I was thankful that I'd brought a heavy jacket with me as I settled into a seat next to Carter. It was going to be a cold ride.

The two men that I hadn't been introduced to were still bustling around, loading their vast amount of stuff onto the boat. They had to get creative since there were already a lot of boxes secured in place with tie-down straps.

One of them, a young African-American man with close-cropped hair, pulled a clipboard out of a bag and stepped toward me. "You're Betty, right? You're perfect, even better-looking than Carter said you were." To my left, I heard a haughty "humph" from Carter, but the man continued. "I'm Dwayne, and that's Mick. I just need you to sign these for me before we get started."

Dwayne pushed the clipboard into my hands, and I squinted in the darkness at the small typing that covered the page clipped to it. There were at least five more pages below it, all covered with the same tiny print. "What is this, a non-disclosure agreement or a waiver of some kind?"

"It's a permission form. For legal reasons, you know."

"Permission for what?"

And that's when I noticed that Mick was pulling something out of a black bag. A video camera.

"Carter, what the hell have you gotten me into?"

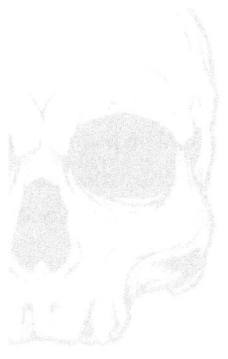

FOUR

Carter at least had the good sense to look mildly ashamed, but he answered, "Oh, did I forget to mention this facet of the investigation? It's being filmed."

"Filmed for what?" My teeth were clenched so tightly that I'm surprised Carter even understood my question.

He understood, and he smiled broadly. "For a new TV show. This is going to be the pilot. Two one-hour episodes about our investigation on the island."

Joseph, who was stationed behind the boat's wheel, let out an amused chuckle. "You didn't know that your friend is the star of a new reality show? Carter, you're more humble than I give you credit for."

"He's not humble. He's sneaky," I said, but I kept my voice low enough that only Carter heard me.

"Betty, you have to sign that paperwork. Otherwise, we can't use any footage with you in it." Carter was speaking to me like I was a child who didn't understand the most basic task.

"I hate you a little bit right now."

"I know. Now sign it."

I thought about refusing, and I considered telling Carter that I'd get off the boat and just take his car back to Savannah. I hated to miss the opportunity to investigate the island, but being filmed every minute was a bad idea. I knew how those shows could make a person look like either a hero or a villain, depending on how the footage was edited, and I suspected that I'd be firmly in the villain category. If Carter was the star of the show, then the producers would want him to have a good foil, someone who questioned his every move and always came out looking like an idiot. That someone was going to be me.

I shook my head and was about to launch into a tirade (since the cameras weren't turned on yet) when Joseph stepped over to me. He squatted down so that we were face to face, and he put his hand on my knee. "Please, Betty. We specifically asked for you because we knew you'd be perfect for this show. You're a good investigator, you're well spoken, and you're the best-looking person here. We need the publicity so we can get enough funding for our project."

"Carter's going to make me look stupid," I said bluntly.

"You do that on your own," Carter said, and I felt my arm twitch in my desire to slap him across the face. "I don't want to make you look stupid. I investigate with you, and that means I trust your opinion in these things. If you look stupid, then I look stupid for having ever teamed up with you. Trust me, you don't have to worry about me trying to make you look bad."

I was silent as I mulled over my decision, and Carter's face looked the tiniest bit worried. He turned to me and lowered his voice. "Please."

"Fine, Carter. Only because you said please." I took the proffered pen from Dwayne and signed my name on the two-hundred (or so it felt) signature lines on the form. I didn't even bother to read all of that fine print, because I already knew that it was full of things I wouldn't like. This had "disaster" written all over it.

The wind whipped across the boat as we sped along the river toward the ocean. Even this far south, it was chilly once the sun went down. The wind felt icy after only five minutes on the water.

"How far do we have to go?" I shouted over the noise.

"Six miles," Joseph answered. That sounded like a short distance, but when you're on a boat, in the dark, and freezing cold, it's a long way to go.

The boat ride to the island was so cold that I soon decided to forgive Carter, at least until we were on dry land again. I pulled the collar of my jacket up and snuggled against him. I would yell at him later about tricking me into being on his reality show, but right now he was a warm body. I was pleased to see that his hair was blowing in the wind, even if it was waving less violently than my own. My hair was only jaw-length, but I knew I'd have nothing but one big auburn knot when we got off the boat.

Hopefully, Mick wouldn't turn on his camera until I'd had a chance to comb it out.

There was no point in trying to talk during the rest of the ride. It was just too loud. Mick tried to do some filming at one point, but the boat was going so fast that every ripple we hit felt like a freight train, and we were bouncing hard enough that I gripped Carter's arm to keep from bouncing right out of my seat. Mick gave up after he, and the camera, nearly fell overboard.

After what seemed like an hour, the boat slowed, and I looked up to see faint lights in the near distance. The island stood out as a black mass against the sky, which was bright with stars and a moon that had passed full just a few days before. It was a bigger island than I'd envisioned, and I felt my original excitement beginning to return. It would be fun to get out and explore the place in the morning.

At the moment, though, my primary concern was warming up. I pried my numb fingers from Carter's arm and stretched. My shoulder muscles were cramped from huddling against Carter.

The lights were quickly growing larger and brighter, and soon I could see the shape of a dock. Rob struggled to get out of the boat and onto the dock so he could tie us to the mooring. As soon as Joseph cut the engine, I jumped up and hauled my suitcase onto the dock by myself. I was hoping it would help get some warmth back into my limbs.

I also helped unload all of the other bags and boxes. Carter stood by idly, and I nudged Dwayne before I hefted a big box labeled "dry goods."

"*That* is what you should be filming," I said, tilting my head toward Carter.

"You two are like oil and water, aren't you?"

"Yes. Carter is the oil because he's slimy."

Dwayne pumped his fist. "Reality show gold! You two are going to be fun to watch."

Joseph instructed Carter and me to follow him once we'd gotten everything unloaded from the boat. We walked slowly along the dock while Joseph pointed out weak spots with a flashlight. "Don't step there," he said, pointing at a rotten board. "Or there. That hole will dump you right into the surf." If the building we were staying in was in as bad of repair as the dock, then I was in for a very long vacation.

A faded wooden sign stood at the end of the dock, and Joseph's flashlight illuminated flaking blue script that read, "Serenity Island Resort, Your Ocean Paradise." We walked up the remains of a path made with old shells, and I could discern the outline of a building ahead of us. There was a soft glow coming from several of the windows, but almost the entire second floor was dark.

Serenity Island Resort had once been magnificent. The building looked like a plantation home, with wide porches across the front of both stories and massive columns that dominated the façade. We trooped up a wide set of sagging, creaking stairs that, I was sure, had once felt the tread of very expensive shoes attached to very rich people.

It was impossible to tell the color of the building in the darkness, but I could see that long tendrils of ivy had grown over large portions of the walls. The windows on either side of the double front doors had broken panes.

Joseph moved with confidence, clearly familiar with the surroundings. He unlocked the front doors and ushered us inside with a grand sweep of his arm. I was wondering why anyone would bother locking the door on a deserted island when Carter stopped short, and I bumped into him. I peeked around him when I heard him exclaim softly.

The room had once been the lobby of the resort, and it was lit with at least a dozen oil lamps. The furniture was still there, and a distinct musty smell wafted from the couch and three overstuffed chairs which surrounded a majestic fireplace on our left. To the right, a dark wood counter marked where employees had once greeted vacationers.

A brass chandelier stretched its long arms above us, and there was some kind of mural painted on the ceiling. Years of neglect and the shadows cast by the oil lamps kept its scene a mystery.

"This is amazing," I said quietly. "It must have been beautiful in its heyday."

"It was," Joseph assured me. "You'll fall in love when you see it in the daylight. Some of the rooms were better protected from the elements over the years and are even more impressive."

Joseph continued walking, and I stepped carefully over chunks of plaster that had fallen from the ceiling. We went up one side of the double staircase that curved up to the second floor, threading our way as carefully as we had on the dock.

When we reached the landing on the second floor, I saw a lot of yellow caution tape strung between the walls leading to the hallway to the right. "The north wing has too many rotten boards to be safe," Joseph warned us. "You'll be staying in the south wing. We've done some basic renovations to the rooms we're all staying in so we can have some semblance of modern comfort."

We walked past a few rooms before Joseph stopped and pointed to a door on the left. "Carter, you can take room 208. Betty, you're in 210."

Joseph opened the door and led me into a spacious room lit by three oil lamps. The floor was a dark hardwood that would probably be beautiful after a thorough cleaning and polishing. A fireplace with an ornate mantle was on one wall, and a simple double bed stood opposite. A small trunk sat underneath the window that looked out onto the second-floor balcony. The door that led out there from my room had been patched with plywood. Otherwise, the room was plain but clean and neat. The walls had been recently whitewashed, and the air lacked the damp, mildewy smell elsewhere in the building.

"We brought over some basic furniture when we first started spending time out here," Joseph explained. "I hope you'll be comfortable. There is no electricity here, but you have plenty of candles, oil lamps, and matches. There's wood in the fireplace already, and more wood can be brought up if you like."

"Thank you," I said. I silently wondered how I was going to survive for two weeks with no electricity. I was a big fan of modern conveniences.

"I do have some bad news to share." Joseph's tone was serious, but the corners of his mouth twitched up. "There's running water here, but the boilers are no longer working. You'll have to take a lot of cold showers, I'm afraid."

That *was* bad news. "That's worse than zombies," I intoned.

Joseph smiled, revealing perfect white teeth. "I'm sure we can find ways to make it tolerable for you."

Thank goodness there were footsteps behind Joseph at that moment, because I'm not sure how I would have replied. Carter stood in the doorway, every hair once again in place.

"Dinner will be at nine. It's in the ballroom directly below this room." With that, Joseph turned and left.

"I have to be on your reality show and take cold showers for the next two weeks," I told Carter. "You really owe me."

"I'm giving you the chance to investigate zombies. I'd think that would make it all worth it." As he spoke, Carter's head turned to follow Joseph's retreat down the hallway.

"I'm surprised that you're willing to stay in such primitive accommodations."

"And I'm surprised that you haven't done anything about your hair yet." Carter stepped forward and tugged gently at a lock of my hair. "We can't have you looking like this on TV."

"Would you care to brush it out for me?" I joked. Carter looked like he was actually considering it. He probably figured that he could do a better job than me. I stepped away and dug through my suitcase for my toilet articles. The hair dryer I had brought would be useless.

I finally found my brush and began carefully working it through my tangles. Carter stood silently, torn between watching me and glancing behind him at the open door to my room. "Just shut it, already," I told him. "What do you expect, that a zombie is going to come shuffling through there?"

"It's not the zombies I'm worried about." Still, Carter shut the door and fastened the latch.

"Then what are you worried about?"

"Nothing." Carter came forward and stared at me. He brought his hand up, and I thought he was going to comment on my hair again, but this time the tips of his fingers came to rest against my jaw.

I got a sudden, horrifying feeling that Carter was going to kiss me. Had Daisy been right about him? Surprised, I gasped and pulled away.

Carter continued to stare at me. "You might want to put on some more make-up, too," he said.

He walked out of my room before I could muster a response.

In the end, I took Carter's advice and touched up my make-up before heading down to the ballroom for dinner. I knew I had made the right choice as soon as I walked in. A long table was set for dinner, with candelabras providing most of the illumination. The table glowed, but the rest of the ballroom was dark. All I could really tell was that it was big. The other light in the room came from Mick's camera. It was glaringly bright, and although I squinted if I looked directly at it, at least I knew I had perfect hair and make-up for any shots Mick got of me.

Joseph was already seated at the head of the table, and he rose to greet me. Carter followed soon after, and Rob completed the group. With Rob seated at the other end of the table, Carter and I each had a side to ourselves. There was room for at least four more people to dine. I asked Dwayne why he was shadowing Mick instead of sitting down to join us, and he gave me some explanation about not wanting to interfere with us. "Just pretend that me, Mick, and the camera aren't even here," he concluded.

Right, because that would be easy.

A woman came bustling into the room then, coming from what must have been the kitchen. She was dressed in black slacks and a simple white button-down blouse, and she was balancing four plates.

"This is Adrienne," Joseph said as the woman put plates of baked chicken in front of us. Dinner looked a lot fancier than I'd expected for a place with no power and no hot water.

"How many preservationists are here?" I asked.

"Just Joseph and me," Rob spoke up. "Adrienne is our housekeeper. We brought in a couple of generators so she could prepare our meals."

Carter looked duly impressed by such service, but I found it a little odd that two guys couldn't handle their own food. I was sure their work to document the island and its renovation needs was exhausting, but still, grilling a couple of chicken breasts shouldn't have been that tough.

The food was really good, though, so I decided that I was okay with their decision to bring a housekeeper all the way to the island.

When our plates were empty, Joseph got up and wandered into a dark corner of the room. He soon returned with a bottle of wine, which he poured liberally for each of us. Adrienne collected our plates while Joseph settled back in his chair. He looked like he was holding court there at the head of the table.

"Serenity Island Resort," he began, "was built in 1946. Americans were feeling really optimistic after the War, and plenty of rich folks were looking for the extravagance they'd been denied for the past several years. A man by the name of Earnest Dowd decided that what people really needed was a remote island where they could forget about their lives on the mainland. He's not the first to make such plans.

"Dowd chose this island because it had milder weather than islands up north, and because he wanted something that wasn't too far from a major port like Savannah. It used to be that families staying on Serenity Island boarded a boat in Savannah. The long ride really made them feel like they were getting away from it all."

Joseph paused and sipped at his wine. "The resort has five buildings that are still standing. The lodge, which is where we are, as well as two cabins that families could rent. The other surviving buildings are a barn, where horses were kept for riding on the beach, and an old chicken coop."

"When did the resort close?" Carter asked.

"Serenity Island was popular throughout the nineteen-fifties, but it began to decline in the sixties as people started to favor air travel and less expensive vacations. It closed in sixty-five, but a couple bought it and reopened the resort a few years later. They were able to bring people out by boat from Darien, like we did tonight. Much of the original luxury remained, but it was marketed to the middle-class as a quiet place to get away. The activities were fewer, the food was simpler, and the service was not nearly as good. It closed for good in seventy-six and has been vacant ever since."

"I'm surprised the buildings haven't been trashed by vandals," I commented. I had been in more than a few haunted buildings that had gotten their fair share of spray paint and smashed windows.

"This island is too remote to be of much worry. A lot of people don't even know it's here. Those who do take the time to come out here are more interested in seeing the old buildings, not in destroying them. A number of items that were left here—room décor, primarily—is gone. We suspect that some visitors wanted to take a souvenir home, assuming that no one would ever miss them."

"You've told me about the zombies, but Betty doesn't know all of the details," Carter prompted.

Joseph sighed and thought for a moment before answering. He had been looking right at us while he spoke, but now his eyes were directed at the table. "We started coming out here a year ago to do our initial surveys. We had to determine if the place was even worth saving. Since then, we've come to the island once every two or three months to do more evaluations. We made a visit the first week of November, and there they were. If they were on the island during prior visits, then we never saw any evidence of them."

"And you think there are actual dead bodies roaming the island?" I asked. I didn't really care if I sounded incredulous.

Joseph nodded.

"Maybe they were apparitions that looked corporeal."

I thought that Joseph would take time to consider my suggestion, but he looked up at me with that same intent stare he'd used before. "They are not apparitions. They are reanimated corpses, and they are wandering this island."

The cold, matter-of-fact tone that Joseph used made me shiver. When Carter talked about zombies, it sounded comical. When Joseph talked about them, it sounded like a very grave matter.

"How many are there?" I asked quietly.

"We've found five so far."

I fell silent, and after a long pause, Joseph drained his glass and set it down with a loud thud. "On that note, I think it's time we all get some rest. Obviously we don't have alarm clocks here, but Adrienne will be around to wake everyone. Tomorrow morning, I'll take you to meet the zombies."

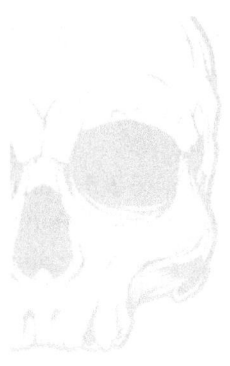

FIVE

How was I supposed to sleep after hearing that story? I had a lot of questions, and a lot of doubts, as we returned to our rooms together. My room was the furthest from the stairs, and soon only Carter and I were left in the hallway.

"You didn't argue with Joseph about the existence of zombies," he noted.

"He seemed to really believe what he was saying. I figure I'll just wait until we see them tomorrow morning before I make up my mind."

"I sure hope the camera is focused on you when we meet them. I want thousands of viewers to see your expression, and then I want them to hear you say that you were wrong, and I was right."

I narrowed my eyes at Carter. "We'll see."

I opened my door and was already stepping across the threshold when Carter spoke softly. "Betty? Lock your door." He paused, then added, "Good night."

"Good night, Carter. I'll see you in the morning."

I did as Carter had instructed and locked my door. It was chilly in my room, so I changed into pajamas quickly and dove under the covers before I remembered that I couldn't just flick a switch to turn off the oil lamps. I got back up, blew out the lamps, and felt my way back to the bed. I could hear the sound of waves crashing against the beach, and their rhythmic beat lulled me to sleep. Despite Joseph's tale of the zombies, I didn't stir until I heard a sharp knock on my door.

When I opened my eyes, sunlight was streaming through the window. The sky was a perfect blue, and I felt a renewed excitement at this venture. It was a beautiful day, I was on vacation, and there were strange paranormal phenomena to investigate.

Adrienne knocked again and called a greeting from the hallway, and I assured her that I was up. I looked at my cell phone, which had the only clock in the room. It was eight o'clock. I noticed that I had no cell coverage this far away from the world and shut my phone off. If I wanted to charge it, I would have to plug it into one of the generators in the kitchen. Since I couldn't make calls, anyway, there was no point in leaving it on.

I wasn't looking forward to my first task of the morning, which was to get through a cold shower. The bathroom had once been lavish, but now there were rust spots on the claw-foot tub, and many of the tiny tiles on the wall had fallen off. I left the bathroom door open for extra light and lit an oil lamp on the countertop.

I turned on the water, took a deep breath, and jumped into the tub. I gave such a loud shout of shock that Carter probably heard it next door. I wet my hair and turned off the shower while I lathered. I turned it back on to rinse, then repeated the same process with my conditioner and soap. It was probably the fastest shower I'd ever taken, but I was shivering when I got out.

After I was dressed and ready to go, I walked out onto the balcony and soaked up the warmth of the sun. The ocean was calm this morning, and a pelican skimmed low over the water's surface as I watched.

I didn't know what time breakfast was or how long I had taken to get ready. I wandered downstairs to the ballroom and found only Joseph seated there, in the same spot as the night before.

"Good morning, Betty," he said, rising from his chair. "I hope you slept well?"

"Very well, thank you."

Joseph motioned to an urn of coffee standing on a sideboard, and at a nod from me, he poured me a cup. "Adrienne takes good care of you and Rob," I said.

"We're going to be out here until Christmas, so we wanted to have some comforts of home."

"It must be difficult for her, being so far away from her family and friends. She's all alone out here with two strangers." I sipped my coffee, wondering what it would be like to be that isolated without a familiar face to see every day.

"She's been working for the society for a long time, and Rob and I are far from strangers to her. Adrienne has been in worse locations, too, I can assure you." Joseph looked at the jeans and light blue knit top that I was wearing. "I hope you brought warmer clothes. I doubt we'll get through the next two weeks without a cold front."

"I brought a jacket and some sweatshirts," I assured him. "I'm more worried about how cold it will get in our rooms with no heat in this place."

"If you can get a good fire going, you'll be too hot in that room. I'll make sure you're comfortable while you're here."

I tipped my head in acknowledgement and took another long sip of coffee. Carter and Rob filed in before I'd finished my cup, and soon we all had plates of scrambled eggs, bacon, and hash browns in front of us.

Carter and I were the first ones to finish eating. I think we were both rushing in our eagerness to see the zombies. I was on my second cup of coffee before Dwayne and Mick came from the direction of the kitchen, where I guessed they were taking their meals.

Once Adrienne cleared the dishes, I assumed we would be on our way. Instead, Dwayne pulled a chair into a shaft of sunlight coming through one of the tall windows at the front of the ballroom. He insisted that Carter and I each sit down for an interview. He wanted to get our opinions of the zombie story before we actually saw any evidence of them. Carter and I were both fitted with little microphones that clipped to our shirts. I fed the wire down the back of my shirt and attached the battery pack to my jeans. It wouldn't be so bad to wear for a few interviews, I decided.

I gave my skeptical view of the zombie claims for the camera, then stood to let Carter have his turn. "Great, Betty," Dwayne told me. "Just keep the mic on for the rest of the day. Only don't forget to turn it off when you go to the bathroom!"

Well, great, every word I said might be captured for posterity. I'd have to watch my mouth, for sure.

As soon as Carter was done, Joseph announced that we'd make the short walk to the barn. "We've collected the zombies that we've found so far in there. They're locked in so they can't escape. I hope you're ready to meet them."

It was about time.

Joseph led the way, striding out of the front doors of the lodge like he was the master of the house. Carter and I followed, and Rob brought up the rear. Dwayne now had a camera, too, and he hustled to get in front of Joseph so he could film us walking toward the barn. I assumed that Mick was somewhere behind us.

An overgrown trail wound into the wooded interior of the island, and after about two hundred yards of stepping over fallen pine trees and dead palm fronds, we came into a small clearing with a rickety barn in the center. The barn had probably never been very nice to begin with, and its wooden beams were really showing their age. There was a hole in one section of the roof, and the entire building looked like it might collapse the next time a hurricane came up the coast.

Joseph unlocked a big padlock on the door of the barn, but instead of opening the door, he turned to us. "Are you prepared for this?" he asked dramatically, gesturing to us to move in closer.

Joseph swung open the door, and I saw a man standing in a shaft of sunlight from the hole in the roof. At a glance, he just looked like a really dirty, sick person.

And then the smell hit me. I turned away and bent over as my stomach lurched. I gagged, praying I wouldn't throw up while there were cameras around. I stepped away from the barn door and kept my head down and my eyes shut, concentrating only on breathing in the fresh sea air.

I had never smelled rotting flesh before. Its concentrated stench had come flooding out of the barn door. I didn't know what Carter's reaction had been, but I knew he must have been horrified by the smell, too.

My eyes caught sight of Mick as soon as I felt recovered enough to look around me. He was crouched down with his camera angled up at my face. I turned my back on him, looking for the others. Carter was holding a hand to his nose, and his jaw was clenched tightly. Joseph and Rob, I noticed, had both pulled out handkerchiefs and had them pressed to their faces.

Joseph caught my eye. "I'm sorry. I should have warned you about the smell." He pulled an extra handkerchief from his pocket and passed it to me.

I pressed the red handkerchief to my nose and mouth. It smelled like it had been sprayed with musky cologne, and I wondered if that was what Joseph wore. It was a nice scent, and I was grateful that I could now approach the barn door without fear of gagging again.

There were now two zombies standing just a few feet inside the door. They had obviously come over in response to us, and I wondered how quickly they were able to move. One was a woman dressed in a tattered gray pantsuit, and the other was a man in jeans and a tee-shirt. His shirt was covered in what looked like old blood, and I wondered if he'd gotten hurt before he'd died, or after.

Because there was no doubt in my mind now that these really were corpses. Their faces were slack, and they had milky eyes that didn't focus on anything. A dark green mold of some kind grew on the woman's arm, and every inch of skin that I could see was oddly discolored. Some patches looked bruised, while others were a flat white. The man's nose had fallen off, leaving a cavity in the middle of his face that reminded me of a skull.

I had thought that vindictive demons were the worst thing I would ever deal with as a ghost hunter. I was wrong. In that instant, I knew I would never again see a paranormal entity so horrifying as these zombies. And yet, there was something pitiful about the walking corpses standing in front of me. These weren't the voracious, brain-eating zombies of Hollywood, these were the terrible cases of lost souls who couldn't find their way to the other side.

"We have to help these people," I said, lifting the handkerchief from my face briefly.

Carter nodded. "I think it's time I told you everything I know about zombies."

We returned to the lodge, and when we were again seated around the dining room table, I looked at Carter and raised my eyebrows.

"What?" he asked.

"Go ahead. Say it."

Carter just smiled wickedly. "Oh, no, I think it would be much better if you say it. Toward the camera, if you please."

"Speaking of which," Dwayne interrupted, "let me get each of you in the chair again for your thoughts on meeting the zombies."

Carter was so eager to hear my response that he took me by the hand and led me to the chair. "You can go first," he said, as if he was granting me a big favor.

When Dwayne gave me the signal that he was ready for me to begin talking, I grimaced as I looked into the camera. "Let's just get it over with," I said dryly. "I was wrong, and Carter was right. Zombies are real, at least in some incarnation."

I started to get up, but Dwayne motioned for me to sit again. "What did you think when you saw them?" he asked.

"I thought I was going to be sick. I also think they are one of the saddest things I've ever seen, and I hope we can help them."

When Carter and I traded places, I stuck my tongue out at him. I made sure my head was turned so that neither camera would catch it.

Carter finished his interview and returned to the table. I was sure he'd given some of this information to Joseph and Rob already. Rob looked bored, and his eyes kept straying to the window. Joseph, on the other hand, split his attention between Carter and me.

"Stories of animated corpses date back thousands of years," Carter said. "The truth about them has been twisted over time, and wild claims have arisen in popular folklore. Those stories gave inspiration to writers, who created fictional characters much worse than the real thing ever was. You were right, Betty, when you said they were sad and need help.

"I confess that calling them zombies is a bit of a misnomer. The proper term is revenant. Medieval folklore talks about people who came back from death to terrorize their friends and family. From the perspective of the living, it *would* seem like you were being terrorized if your dead uncle suddenly walked into your house. Most people were too scared, and too superstitious, to stop and consider the reasons a corpse might come back from the dead."

"Why would they come back?" I asked.

"For the same reasons ghosts hang around instead of crossing over. Some don't know they are dead, some have unfinished business. They might be scared of crossing over or are just too happy here to want to move on. With revenants, you can typically trace their presence to unfinished business or the belief that they're still alive."

Carter's words began to click into place. "We are dealing with ghosts, then," I surmised. "Instead of haunting a house or an object, like an antique bed, they're haunting their own bodies."

Carter nodded his head approvingly. "Exactly. They weren't ready to die for one reason or another, and the spirit has tried to re-enter the body. Once that initial connection has been broken, though, there's no way to get it back. The result is just a mockery of life."

"We have to help these spirits cross over," I said. I had seen Carter convince a ghost to cross over after only a few minutes of persuasion. With his smooth talking to the spirits, I figured we'd have this whole thing wrapped up by sundown.

"It's why we're here, but it won't be easy."

"Why not? You've done this sort of thing before."

"Exactly. And I know from my work in Mexico that zombies are a lot harder to cross over than ghosts. They have to impart information before they're willing to go or get answers that they're looking for. In the case of souls who don't know they're dead, well, there we're just facing a really stubborn attitude."

Now that I knew they were ghosts, I felt more confident about my ability to deal with the zombies, provided I could approach them without getting knocked over by the smell. Still, if Carter said we had our work cut out for us, then I believed him.

"What do we need to do first?" I asked. "Can they talk to us, or do we need to have an EVP session?"

"EVP works better. Ghosts don't have a lot of control over their bodies, so just walking is a difficult task. Forming the mouth and tongue—if it's still intact—into words requires too much precision to be practical."

"Rob and I will help in any way we can," Joseph said. "We've got plenty of site research to conduct, but we're happy to help you with your investigation."

"It would be nice to have you with us for the first few sessions. I think Betty will be more comfortable if it's not just two humans trying to talk to five zombies. Actually, we need a way to pull them away from the group, one at a time, so we can talk to them."

Joseph promised he could help us corral them. We still had a couple of hours to kill before lunch, so we decided to start right away. Carter and I grabbed our tape recorders, and we made the trek to the barn for the second time that morning.

This time, I felt much better prepared. Joseph's handkerchief was firmly pressed against my face before he'd even unlocked the barn door.

Joseph and Rob had already devised a system for moving the zombies around. They had long poles that looked like they had once had nets attached for cleaning a swimming pool. A loop of rope was attached to the end of each pole. Joseph and Rob slid their ropes around the closest zombie—the woman in the gray pantsuit—and guided her outside.

It was slow going, but inch by inch, the two men steered the woman into a small fenced area adjacent to the barn. We had decided that, although being outdoors meant there might be background noise in our EVP sessions, it was best to do our work where the smell would be diluted.

"We can hold her here if it makes you more comfortable," Rob offered. He had his pole tucked under his arm so he could adjust his wide-brimmed hat. Clearly, he was used to being around the walking dead and saw little need for caution.

Carter looked significantly at me, but I just shrugged. "You can let her go," I said. "I'm not worried that she'll chase me down."

A chunk of the woman's scalp came off, dangling limp strands of dark brown hair, when Rob lifted the rope over her head. He couldn't have grazed her skin that hard with the rope, but it was enough. I shut my eyes and turned away. When I opened them, Carter was looking at me with worry.

"That's disgusting," I whispered.

"I would say that you'll get used to it, but I'd be lying." Carter actually looked a little sympathetic. He gave me a reassuring squeeze on my arm and returned his attention to the zombie. Carter pulled his tape recorder out of his pocket, turned it on, and held it just inches from the zombie's mouth. I involuntarily reached out to grab the back of his shirt, as if I might have to snatch him to safety at any moment.

The zombie, though, just stood there, still and mute.

"My name is Carter, and this is Betty. We are here to help you." Carter had raised his voice so that he was nearly shouting. I didn't know if he thought the ghost inside the decaying body was hard of hearing or if he was just determined to get his message across the first time. "What is your name? Where are you from? Do you know that you are dead?"

Carter went through the standard list of EVP questions, pausing between each. I found myself listening for words to come out of the zombie's mouth and reminded myself that I wouldn't hear any responses just yet. After all, we usually didn't hear anything until we went through our audio recordings. Recorders often picked up voices that we couldn't hear with our own ears during the session.

If the woman was giving us answers, then she was doing it spectrally, not physically. The only time she opened her mouth was when Carter said, "Wow, they really stink up close." Then, the woman's lips pushed forward. A burbling sound erupted, slow and monotone.

"I think you offended her," I said.

Carter responded by handing me his tape recorder. "You take over. I need some fresh air."

I was hesitant about stepping as close to the woman as Carter had. I wasn't afraid, just a little grossed out. Standing face-to-face with a rotting corpse is enough to give anyone pause. I much preferred ghosts because they couldn't be seen, heard, or smelled. At least, not like this.

Carter had already covered the typical questions, but I ran through the list again. Ghosts sometimes respond better to a particular person, so maybe one of us would get results that the other didn't.

The tape recorder's timer had reached the twenty-minute mark before I finally gave up. I looked at Carter questioningly. "I don't think there's any more we can do right now," I said.

"Time for the next one. Joseph, Rob, would you two be so kind as to get us a new zombie?"

After Lady Gray, as I was referring to her in my head, was shuffled back to the barn, Joseph and Rob returned with a man roped between them. It was the first one I had seen, standing in the sunlight. His pants and shirt were ripped and filthy, and his protruding belly was oddly lumpy. Unkempt hair and a thick beard hid most of his purple-hued face, and I was grateful for that small reprieve.

I figured this one should be called Beard, but giving him a nickname struck a thought. "Has anyone checked their pockets for I.D. or something that might help us identify them?" I asked.

"Help yourself," Carter said.

There was absolutely no way I was going to stick my hand into that guy's pants pocket. Snippets of every horror movie I'd ever seen flashed through my mind in seconds.

I had thought I wasn't scared, but I was kidding myself. I was perfectly brave only as long as I was out of arm's reach.

Joseph proved to be the bravest—or craziest—one of the bunch. He laid down the end of his pole and walked right over to the zombie. Beard barely stirred when Joseph began searching his pockets. There was nothing to be found, anyway.

I started the EVP session this time, and Carter asked the second round of questions. When we were done, Joseph and Rob began to lead Beard away.

About halfway back to the barn, I heard a wet ripping sound. Rob shouted a few swear words, and even Joseph backed as far away as the pole would allow.

"What happened?" Carter called.

"Just stay where you are," Joseph said. But already Beard was turning around so that we could see what had made that awful sound. The skin of his belly had burst open, and a mixture of dark, wet goo and big chunks of tissue were sliding down the front of his pants.

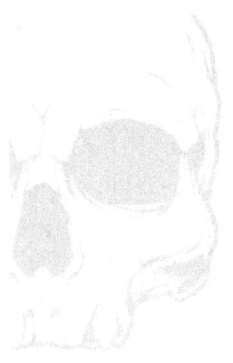

SIX

This time, it didn't matter if there were any cameras trained on me or not. I turned away from Carter and threw up.

The walk back to the lodge was just a blur. I was filled with a mixture of absolute disgust and extreme embarrassment. Carter sat me down in a dining room chair and disappeared for a moment. When he came back, he pushed a bottle of water into my hand and implored me to drink. I was shaking so badly that I could barely comply.

I took a few sips before I gave up and handed the bottle back to Carter. I bent forward and cradled my head in my hands. I wanted to cry, but I'd been mortified enough for one day.

"I'm so sorry," I whispered.

"Sorry for what?" I heard a chair scrape across the hardwood floor and felt Carter sit down next to me. He put one arm around my shoulders. "You had a perfectly normal reaction."

"That was the most awful thing I've ever seen in my life. It was worse than seeing Maxwell incinerate people."

"I have to agree with you there. Zombies aren't for the squeamish, but that was worse than even I'm used to. Look on the bright side: at least it didn't happen while you were conducting the EVP session."

I just groaned and swallowed the bile I felt rising in my throat.

Carter was content to quietly sit and keep me company, which was all I wanted. He shifted his arm so that he could stroke my hair, and I felt the gentle motion calming my nerves.

We had a few minutes of peace before I heard footsteps and a voice called, "You are one lucky lady."

"Why?" I asked weakly. I recognized Mick's voice, so I didn't bother to raise my head.

"I was changing out my tape, and Dwayne was filming the zombie. We missed your whole little episode."

That made me feel a bit better. My pride had just taken a serious beating, and I was relieved that I wouldn't have to relive that moment months later, when the show eventually aired on TV. "Oh, good."

Mick's comment reminded me that my body mic was still on. I reached behind me and fumbled with the power switch. It clicked off just as Carter leaned in close to my ear. "He is filming now, though," he whispered.

That was my cue to keep my head down and my mouth shut. I took a few deep breaths and felt my stomach finally settling back into its normal state.

Joseph and Rob made their way into the dining room once they had taken care of Beard. I wasn't sure what that had entailed, and I didn't want to know. "How are you feeling, Betty?" Rob asked. "It's nearly lunchtime. Do you want to eat?"

"No, thank you." I sat up. "I'll go lie down for a while."

"Oh, damn, girl." Mick was staring at me with his mouth open, the camera forgotten for the moment. "You're as pale as death."

"Come on, I'll walk you up to your room," Joseph offered. He took me by the elbow and helped me up.

"Thank you," I said to Carter as I stood. I don't know

if he heard me or not. He was looking at Joseph with narrowed eyes, a frown on his face.

Joseph was quiet as he slowly walked me up the stairs and to the door of my room. Before he left me, though, he said, "I'm sorry you had such a difficult introduction to zombies. I certainly didn't invite you to our island with the intent of upsetting you."

"It's not your fault. I just…wasn't prepared for that." I wasn't sure anyone could ever be prepared for something like that, but I'd been the only one of the group to get physically ill. This investigation was not off to a good start.

I brushed my teeth before curling up in bed. I didn't sleep, but the quiet and solitude made me feel much better.

I emerged from my bedroom a few hours later and was on my way downstairs when Carter's door opened. "You have to hear this!" he said, waving me inside.

Carter had already downloaded our audio recordings to his laptop (I don't know how ghost hunters ever got by before digital recorders), and he had just finished listening to our session with Lady Gray. The laptop was sitting on Carter's bed, so I sat down next to him. "What do you have?"

"I think you'll be excited. Here." I put on the headphones Carter handed me but had to take them off when he started speaking again. "How are you feeling, anyway?"

"Much better," I said.

"You look much better. I was worried that you might pass out on me before."

"So was I. Let's get to the EVP, already."

"Right. We got three interesting responses. Here's the first."

Carter's voice came blaring out of the headphones.

"What is your name?" A quiet, feminine voice answered with a breathy, "Please."

I repeated the word to Carter, who agreed that was the same word he had heard. "Try the second."

Now my own voice said, "Do you want us to help you?" There was a hissing noise that followed, but it was difficult to hear. "That's inconclusive," I told Carter. "It almost sounds like she's saying yes to us, but it could just as easily be the wind in the trees."

"I thought it was a pretty clear answer."

"Good thing we're allowed to disagree with each other. Play the third, please."

The third time was the charm with Lady Gray. After I asked if she knew she was dead, her quiet voice distinctly said, "Not dead, not dead."

"Wow. Great EVP!"

Carter nodded enthusiastically. "And great news, because it means she should cross over pretty easily. We just have to convince her that she's dead."

I looked up to check the time, but of course, there was no clock in the room. I didn't know what time it was, but the sun was still shining brightly outside. "Do you want to work with her this afternoon? It would be nice to cross one zombie off our list on our first day."

"Are you sure you're ready to go back out there?"

My head moved up and down, but my answer was, "I'm not sure. It's better just to dive back into it, right? Face your fears and all that."

"Just don't eat before you go."

I smacked Carter's arm for that one.

Since Carter had gone over Lady Gray's EVP session, I offered to sift through Beard's. Picturing him standing there in front of me made me a little queasy again, but I tried to push the feeling to the back of my mind. If I couldn't toughen up, then it was going to be a terrible two weeks.

While I sat with the headphones on, Carter laid back with his hands behind his head. He stared up at the ceiling until I suddenly jumped. "What is it?" he asked, sitting up.

"I'm not sure." I handed him the headphones and cued the recording.

Carter listened intently. I played the recording a second time. He shook his head. "I know what it sounds like, but it's not. There's no way it could be."

Of course, Carter was right. The noise sounded just like the faint "pop" that always announced the materialization of a demon.

"We were out in the open, and he would have to have been really close by for the recorder to pick up that sound. It's probably a tree branch snapping in the distance." Carter handed the headphones back to me. "I'm sorry, Boo."

"I think my brain is just a little scrambled after our adventure this morning," I conceded. "Hopefully the next thing I find on here will be a real EVP."

I had no such luck. Maybe Beard was too distracted by his impending rupture to answer us, or maybe his spirit hadn't figured out how to communicate yet. At least we had made progress with Lady Gray.

Carter was staring up at the ceiling again, and his gaze didn't shift when I asked, "How come these bodies aren't buried in a cemetery somewhere?"

"Clearly they never received a proper burial. Maybe they lived alone, died, and reanimated before anyone found them. Or, for those with unfinished business, it could have been a hit and run accident on a little-used road, an unsolved murder, even a suicide. It's a lot easier to learn their history when you know where they came from. In Mexico, we suspected from the start that the three we were dealing with had been killed by a drug cartel."

I lay back and gazed above me, too, hoping the ceiling would offer the same enlightenment for me. "That brings up a second question. How do five zombies wind up on an uninhabited island? I seriously doubt we're dealing with the remnants of Gilligan and his friends."

"Someone would have had to bring them here," Carter concluded. "Who or why, I don't know."

There was no evidence left to review, and we had plenty of time before sundown, so I couldn't put off going back to the barn. Joseph and Rob joined us again, and I trailed behind the three men as we walked into the clearing. I stood by the fence and waited as Lady Gray was escorted over.

Even with Joseph's handkerchief pressed tight against my nose and mouth, I could smell the decay emanating from Lady Gray. Either my nose was more sensitive after my "episode," as Mick had called it, or the cologne on the handkerchief was wearing off.

Still, I was doing okay until Carter and I moved in closer. My feet suddenly stopped moving. "I don't know if I can do this," I said quietly.

"Stay behind me. You'll be fine." Carter glanced significantly at Dwayne. He wanted me to put on a brave face for the camera. Facing a zombie again was something I needed to do for myself, too, so I took a deep breath of fresh air and followed Carter.

Carter has an amazing talent for getting spirits to cross over. He had written about his success in his book (which, for the record, I have never read), and I'd seen it first-hand when he coaxed a dead factory worker into moving on. As far as I'm concerned, I'm a better ghost hunter than Carter. I have more patience and better intuition. But, in this arena, Carter was the clear winner. It hurt to admit that, but it was true.

Carter's voice rose as it had in the morning. "You are dead," he said firmly. "I know that you are still conscious and still in your body, but you are dead. Your body is decomposing, and you can't control your body like you could when you were alive. It's time for you to let go. You need to accept that you are dead and cross over."

Lady Gray stood mute, as she had all morning. It was impossible to know if the message was getting across.

Carter glanced at Joseph and Rob. "Take the ropes off her," he instructed. "We'll be okay." As soon as Lady Gray was free of the restraints, I sidestepped so that I was almost completely hidden by Carter. I peeked around the side of his arm to watch the proceedings.

"If you understand me," Carter continued, "then I want you to walk toward me."

Lady Gray took a slow, unsteady step forward.

"Thank you. Now, you should see a light. You probably hear friends and family calling to you. Go toward that light. Give up your body and go to the light. It is a better place. Your body will be whole, and you will be happy. Go to it. Cross over and join the people you love."

There was a long pause. I don't think any of us even breathed as we waited so see what would happen.

Lady Gray collapsed into Carter's arms.

I jumped back with a scream, but Carter moved sideways, and Lady Gray's limp body fell forward. I had already backed up against the fence, and I couldn't go any further. Her rotting head landed with a dull, hollow sound on the sand at my feet.

I leaped over the body and put a few feet between us. I thought I was going to be sick again until I caught sight of

Carter. His face was contorted with disgust, and he held his arms out to his sides like he was trying to take flight. I snickered.

"At least her insides aren't on the outside like the other guy," I said.

Carter swallowed hard, and I could almost see his conscious effort to smooth his features back into their normal, self-assured arrangement. "I was successful. She crossed over."

"Which means we can check her off the list. Well done, both of you," Joseph said.

"I hate to say it, but Carter gets the credit for this one." I looked down at Lady Gray, who had landed face-first in the sand. "Now, what do we do with the dead body?"

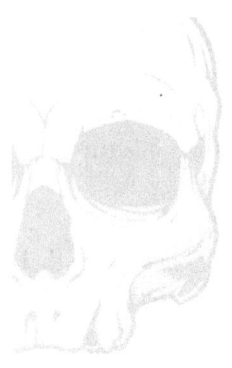

SEVEN

In the end, we decided to bury Lady Gray at the edge of the clearing, on the far side of the barn. The men rolled her up in a tarp and dragged her over to the gravesite. I pitched in with the digging but refused to go near the body.

The sun was setting as we put the final layer of dirt over Lady Gray's grave. The sky was a deep blue with hues of purple, and the shadows were quickly closing in around the clearing.

It felt sneaky to bury Lady Gray. Sure, she was dead long before we came across her, but hiding her away like this felt wrong. She probably had family members somewhere who missed her. They would never know what had become of her. Even now, they might be putting up missing-person posters or organizing one final search to look for her body. It was too bad we didn't have any way of identifying her so we could help her family and friends get some closure.

The last glow of daylight was quickly fading behind the tree line as we trooped back to the lodge. We were all sweaty and dirty, though Carter took the prize for having actually come into contact with a zombie. I suspected he'd take an extra-long shower with lots of scrubbing.

We wended our way down the trail, walking slowly to

avoid tripping over the fallen trees and branches. Joseph hadn't brought his flashlight along since we never expected to be in the clearing for so long. We were all introspective on the walk, and when we parted to go to our rooms, the only words came from Joseph, who told us that it was a quarter after six, and dinner would be served at eight.

I had expected to feel my way through my dark room, and I was pleasantly surprised to find a small blaze in the fireplace. By the time I got a few oil lamps burning, the room was positively glowing. It had a warm, romantic feel, and I felt a little sad that Maxwell wasn't there to share it with me. I realized with a start that it was the first time I'd thought about Maxwell in hours. I'd been too absorbed with Lady Gray all afternoon to think of anything else.

Rotting bodies aside, coming to Serenity Island was already proving to be good for me. Maybe I'd finally be able to get over Maxwell completely. Carter was so good at getting spirits to move on, and I wished that he could use that same skill to get me to move on. It would be nice if a few smooth words could make everything all right in an instant.

The cold shower felt almost good after the hard work I'd put into the grave digging. The tightness in my shoulders promised that I'd be sore in the morning, but I felt refreshed after my shower. I headed downstairs when I was dressed in clean clothes, but the dining room was empty. Instead, I wandered out to the front porch of the lodge.

The moon had risen enough to cast a soft white light over the landscape, and I could see it reflecting off the ripples in the ocean. I leaned my elbows against the porch rail and breathed deeply. I love the smell of the salty air. One of the downsides of being a ghost hunter is the nocturnal hours on weekends. I almost never got to the beach on Tybee Island anymore, and I missed the ocean.

My thoughts turned again to Lady Gray and anyone

who might still be searching for answers to her disappearance. That scenario was probably similar for all five zombies. I wondered how many bodies never found their way home, even if their spirits moved on. It was a sobering thought.

I heard soft footsteps behind me and felt someone's presence at my side. A hand on my back reminded me of Carter's comforting earlier. "It's been an interesting first day," I said, without turning my head.

"You two certainly dive in headfirst."

Startled, I turned to see Joseph standing next to me. He had changed into jeans and a tight black tee-shirt that showed off his muscles. I could smell the same cologne that was on the handkerchief he'd given me.

I returned my gaze to the ocean, though I was tempted to take another look at Joseph's physique. I gauged he was somewhere in his early to mid-thirties, easily a decade older than me. Still, he was awfully handsome.

"Investigating with Carter is always an adventure," I said.

"What's the story with you two? Carter asked for separate rooms, so obviously you're not seriously involved."

"We're not involved at all. Carter and I just team up for investigations from time to time."

Joseph was quiet for a moment, and I was very conscious of his hand still resting against my back. I wanted to move away, but I didn't want to seem rude. His touch felt very forward to me, but for all I knew, he was just being friendly. "Are you seeing anyone?" Joseph asked.

"I was. We broke up."

"I find it hard to believe that anyone would let you get away easily."

"It's complicated. He had some people after him, and he felt like it was unsafe for me if I was with him."

Joseph laughed derisively. "What, was he mafia or something?"

I paused. "Just a trouble-maker, I guess." Maxwell was definitely trouble, so I was technically telling the truth.

"I once had a girlfriend who stalked me after I broke up with her. She followed me out to an old gold-mining town that we were working to restore. She just showed up one day, out there in the middle of the desert. You've got to watch out for exes."

"I know what you mean. I think he was following me around for a while, just to make sure I was okay, I guess."

"At least you don't have to worry about him following you here."

I nodded. "That's part of the reason I agreed to this crazy idea. Believe me, taking off with Carter for two weeks on a remote island is not something I'd normally do."

"But aren't you glad you did?" Carter's voice came from the doorway behind us.

I craned my neck around. "I'm not sure yet." Joseph's hand, I noticed, was still between my shoulder blades.

I was suddenly very conscious of the tableau that Joseph and I must be presenting to Carter, and I straightened and turned around. "Is it dinner time?" I asked, moving toward the dining room before anyone could answer.

The atmosphere at dinner was a strange one. We were at once celebratory and subdued. I think everyone was physically and mentally worn out from the day's adventure. Joseph poured the wine liberally again and toasted to our quick success with the first zombie.

After I put my glass down, I said, "I have just one

request. Can we not call them zombies? It seems too... impersonal. Too Hollywood."

"Do you prefer the term 'revenants'?" Joseph asked.

"I think so. I associate zombies with soulless creatures, which these definitely are not."

"You can call them anything you like, as long as you and Carter can get them taken care of," Rob joined in. He rarely spoke, and his soft voice was always a little surprising to hear.

I cleaned my plate. Adrienne had served us salmon filets, and I didn't realize how hungry I was until the first buttery bite. I had skipped lunch, and I definitely made up for the missed meal.

Between the wine and the food, I was ready to fall into bed when we went upstairs. Instead of wishing me a good night again, Carter looked at me keenly. "We'll do EVP sessions with the rest of the zombies tomorrow," he said.

"Revenants."

"Whatever. Don't hide behind me the whole time like you did today."

Carter went into his room, leaving me to stare at his door with my mouth agape. After I'd done EVP sessions with both Lady Gray and Beard, I couldn't believe Carter was calling me out for being timid during our afternoon's work. He was even the one who had told me to stand behind him! I would have said all of that to him if he hadn't already gone into his room. I considered knocking on his door and demanding that he let me defend myself, but it wasn't worth it. An argument with Carter was not how I wanted to end my day.

I went straight to bed and slept soundly. The bitter thoughts I was thinking about Carter kept any nightmares about Beard at bay. When I got to breakfast in the morning, Carter was already seated. I placed my hands on the table and leaned toward him. "I hope you're in a better mood than you were last night," I said.

"I was in a fine mood last night."

"For the record, Carter, I only stayed behind you when we were trying to get that zomb—I mean revenant—to cross over. Besides, you didn't need my help for that."

Okay, so I hadn't wanted to end my day with an argument, and here I was starting my day with one. Carter knew how to get under my skin better than anyone I knew.

"Duly noted," Carter said, his tone icy.

"We have got to get the two of you trained." The voice came from behind me, and it belonged to Dwayne. He had a camera in his hand and a frown on his face. "You need to put on your mic before you start squabbling with each other. They'll be in the kitchen, plugged into one of the power strips from the generator, each morning. Go get yours, turn it on, and use the damn thing."

I pouted all the way to the kitchen and all the way back. At least I was nice enough to retrieve Carter's mic for him, even if I did throw it at his head.

Joseph managed to perk me up a little while we ate. His excitement at our early success was contagious, and by the time we left the lodge, I was almost looking forward to working with the next revenant.

Joseph and Rob roped the one I had seen standing with Lady Gray in the barn. The dried blood on his shirt wasn't nearly as disgusting to me after what I'd witnessed the day before, but the cavity where his nose had once been looked a lot worse in the sunlight. I volunteered to ask the first round of questions, determined to prove Carter wrong about me. When I addressed the revenant I was thinking of as Nosy, I had to keep my eyes focused on his shoulder instead of his face.

Even with Carter asking the same questions, the EVP session lasted less than half an hour. It was strange investigating this way. I was used to spending hours investigating a single haunting, doing multiple EVP sessions, taking pictures, and getting video. With a typical ghost, you rarely got a sense of whether it was actually present at any given time. You had to make multiple efforts to contact it in the hopes that at least one attempt would be successful. In this case, though, we knew that each spirit was present as we questioned it. There was no need for photos since the spirit had chosen to reanimate its body rather than going a more traditional route. We wouldn't be seeing any apparitions or catching any objects mysteriously moving on their own.

We didn't need video, either. Dwayne and Mick were both nice guys, but I was already growing weary of having a camera pointed at me every minute. I hoped that I'd get used to it and forget about their presence after a few days.

The two revenants we hadn't questioned yet were brought out one at a time once we finished with Nosy. Granny was an elderly woman who looked surprisingly fresh. Her polka-dot dress still had clean patches, and her wispy gray hair was still pulled up in a bun. She moved really slowly, but given her age, she might have been slow when she was alive, too.

Redneck was a younger guy, probably about my age. He had blonde hair that looked even lighter compared to the dark splotches on his face. Redneck's camouflage overalls had a hole in the chest, and the hole was ringed with a lot of dried blood.

"We think he might have died in a hunting accident," Joseph said.

"I think you're right, Stryker. Someone shot him and left his body out in the woods," Carter speculated. "I wonder if he was shot on purpose, or if it was an accident? We'll include that question in our EVP session. This zombie could be looking for justice."

When we had concluded with those two, I assumed

we'd head back to the lodge. Instead, Carter looked at me and raised his eyebrows. "Are you ready?"

"For what?"

"We didn't get a single EVP from your buddy yesterday. We need to talk to him again."

I slowly let out my breath, wondering if I could face Beard again without giving a repeat performance. "I might let you do the talking," I admitted.

"No surprise there." Carter motioned to Rob. "Can you two bring him out, please?"

Beard still looked like something from the goriest of horror movies. As he shuffled from the barn to the enclosure, a long string of entrails swung in time with his movements. The open wound where his skin had split open still looked slick and wet.

I was definitely not ready. I resisted the urge to turn my head away, but I focused my eyes on Joseph instead of Beard. It was a much pleasanter view.

Carter pulled out his tape recorder and spoke to Beard, asking the same questions that we had posed to the others. When he was done, he turned toward me. "Are you sure you don't want to try?"

"I'm sure." I hated to wimp out. It would look bad on camera, and I'd definitely hear no end of it from Carter. I didn't know why he was pulling the holier-than-thou attitude with me all of a sudden—I'd thought we were past that point in our tenuous friendship—but this would only add fuel to the fire. More importantly, I was disappointing myself. I'm not the type to back down from investigations. I'd been willing to face a spiteful demon in a home in Thunderbolt, but I wasn't willing to look at something to which the average medical student was inured.

We were done with our EVP sessions for the day, which meant our afternoon would be spent reviewing our recordings. I only picked at my lunch before Dwayne pulled me over to the side for an interview about the morning's work.

"How are you and Carter getting along?" he prompted.

"Fine."

Dwayne lowered the camera. "A quick tip about interviewing: repeat the question as part of your answer. You should say, 'Carter and I are getting along fine.' Except you shouldn't say that, because clearly it's not true."

I crossed my legs and folded my arms across my chest. "Carter and I are getting along just fine."

It wasn't what Dwayne wanted to hear, but he was going to have to live with it. He got better material from Carter during his interview. One side of Carter's lip curled up as he answered, "Betty and I are getting along, as always. I've been investigating a lot longer than she has, so it's inevitable that some things will make her squeamish. I'm trying to toughen her up."

Boy, did I hate hearing Carter use the experience angle. Yes, he'd been investigating longer than me, but that was only because he was a few years older. He'd had a head start.

My attitude toward Carter was cool as we settled on his bed to begin reviewing our audio recordings. If he was going to play the arrogant snob, then there was no point in being nice to him.

Five minutes later, I tore off the headphones and grabbed Carter's hands.

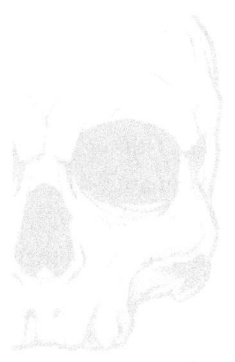

EIGHT

My intuition had kicked into high gear when I heard the first EVP, and it was telling me that something was very wrong. I also knew that I wanted Carter on my side, however much of a jerk he could be.

"Something's not right," I said.

Carter had been lying down, and I was hovering over him so he couldn't sit up. His eyes widened at my outburst, and he squeezed my hands. "Tell me."

I moved so Carter could sit up and listen to the EVP for himself. Nosy hadn't responded to the first few questions I had asked him, but he'd gotten downright chatty when I'd asked, "How did you die?" Carter shut his eyes and clamped his hands over the headphones to listen to the clip, and I knew he'd clearly heard Nosy's answer when he turned sharply to me. "What the hell?" he said.

Carter played the response three more times before he took off the headphones.

"Something is not right about this scenario," I said again, and I knew from Carter's grim demeanor that he agreed completely.

When I had asked Nosy how he died, his response was firm. "The demon did it. They couldn't save me."

"Your ex-boyfriend aside, demons aren't common," Carter said. "Of all the investigations I've been on, maybe four or five of them have been demonic. What are the chances that one of our zombies died at the hands of a demon?"

I tapped my fingers against the laptop as I thought. "Is death by a demon more likely to create a revenant?"

"I doubt it. If someone dies at a demon's hands, it's unlikely that they were even aware what kind of entity they were dealing with in the first place."

"Something is wrong here, Carter." I didn't want to sound like a broken record, but it was worth repeating. "It's weird enough that five revenants are just wandering around an uninhabited island, but now we've got one that died at the hands of a demon. When he said 'they' couldn't save him, who did he mean? If he was with others when he died, they should have taken care of the body. Nosy should be in a coffin right now."

"Who?"

"Ah, I named him Nosy."

"Brilliant. You're not cool with calling them zombies, but you named the guy Nosy."

"Don't start being mean to me again," I said. It came out sounding a lot more pitiful than I had intended. "I think our work is going to involve a lot more than just crossing over these souls. I want to know where they came from and how a demon fits into this. I don't need another one in my life."

"I wasn't mean to you. And yes, you're right. We need to sort this out. It will be great for the show."

I chewed on a fingernail absently. "For now, though, can we keep this information between us? I'm not sure I want to share it with Joseph and Rob just yet."

"Why not?"

"Because I feel like someone isn't being honest with us. Until we know who, I don't want to share this with anyone."

"Fine by me. Do you want to keep listening, or should I take over for a while?" Carter reached for the headphones before waiting for my answer. I was happy to let him listen to the remainder of Nosy's EVP session while I mulled over the implications of what we had heard. I had thought I was done with demons forever, but my instincts were telling me otherwise.

At dinner that night, Joseph asked how our review of the EVP sessions had gone. Carter and I glanced at each other before he answered, "Fairly well, actually." He briefly filled Joseph and Rob in on what we'd found, leaving out Nosy's mention of a demon.

Nosy had given us two more brief responses, which Carter relayed over our bowls of Brunswick stew. We got a "yes" when Carter asked Nosy if he knew he was dead and a strange "aaaahhhh" when Carter introduced himself.

The only EVP we got from Redneck was a garbled sound when Carter asked him who had shot him. We hoped that a future session would yield an actual name, and that maybe Redneck was only waiting to pass on the name of his killer before crossing over.

Granny hadn't yielded any information, but Carter and I both suspected that she simply didn't realize she had died. Foul play just didn't seem like a likely option for her reanimation.

And Beard was still maintaining a stubborn silence. I had decided that I disliked him. I hadn't known it was possible for a revenant to be annoying, but Beard pulled it off.

"Tomorrow morning then, I guess you'll try to send Granny home?" Rob was peering at me over his glasses. It was amusing how quickly the others had adopted my nicknames for the revenants.

"Yes, and then we can continue the EVP sessions."

"This schedule is working out well," Joseph

commented. "It leaves the afternoons free for Rob and me to do our real work. If you'll excuse me, I think I'm turning in early tonight."

We all rose to head upstairs, and Carter again wished me a good night. It was a much nicer way to end my day than the attitude he had given me the night before.

Something woke me with a start in the middle of the night. I thought it was just a dream and turned over, but a sharp knock sounded three times on my door. "Who is it?" I called.

"Rob."

I had no idea what time it was, but I knew it had to be late. I had been dead asleep before Rob's knock. I cracked the door a few inches and saw the hallway beyond illuminated by Rob's flashlight. His face was concerned. "They're loose," he said.

"Who?"

"Them."

"What?" I was not awake enough for this conversation. "Start over and speak in whole sentences, please."

"The zombies have escaped from the barn."

That I could follow. Why couldn't Rob just have said that from the start? "How did you find out?"

Rob shrugged. "I couldn't sleep so I went out for a walk on the beach. I nearly ran into Beard before I saw him. I checked the barn, and it looks like they pulled a few boards out so they could escape. Only Granny was still inside."

"We need to patch up the barn first." Joseph's voice came from the head of the stairs, and he soon joined us. I banged on Carter's door, and we filled him in. I noticed with little surprise that his hair was perfect, and I wondered if he had combed it after he got out of bed.

"As slowly as they move, they can't have gone too far," Carter said.

"We'll divide up and look for them," Joseph said. "First, we'll take some spare pieces of lumber to the barn. Everyone get dressed and meet downstairs in ten minutes."

We all complied, and soon I was wearing jeans and a sweatshirt and questioning the idea of searching for the revenants in the dark. I guess it would be easier to find them before they had time to stray far from the barn, but I still didn't like the idea.

Joseph and Rob had gathered tools, boards, and flashlights. As we walked down the trail to the barn, I kept swinging my flashlight left and right, expecting to see cloudy eyes staring out at me from the underbrush. I checked the trail behind us a few times, but I knew we were moving faster than the revenants could if one decided to follow us.

Granny was still inside the barn, but as Rob had said, a few boards near the door had been pried away. It must have been a tight squeeze for Beard.

The repairs went quickly. Carter and I held the flashlights aloft to provide light while Joseph and Rob got the boards placed over the hole. With that task completed, it was time to round up the revenants. Joseph and Rob retrieved their poles.

"Betty, you come with me," Joseph instructed. "Carter, you and Rob will team up."

Carter didn't look happy about the pairing, but I was glad to be with the man who showed the most competence when dealing with the revenants. If I had to be wandering revenant-infested woods in the middle of the night, then I was happy I was doing it with Joseph.

Rob and Carter went in the direction of the lodge,

leaving Joseph and me to follow a path behind the barn. It led to the guest cabins along the mainland side of the island. Joseph and I both swept our flashlights around us as we walked slowly down the path.

"They really have been misbehaving since you and Carter arrived," Joseph said. "We had no problems from them before. Since you arrived, Beard has decided to rot in the worst way possible, and now they've escaped."

"I don't think Beard was acting intentionally. As for the escape, maybe it does have to do with Carter and me. Now that someone is trying to speak to them and struggling to interact, it could be prompting the spirits to increase their activity. Maybe this is some way of attempting to communicate."

"An interesting theory."

We fell silent for a short time. "How long were you and your ex together?" Joseph suddenly asked.

"Not long. Only about a month."

"And yet he's been following you? He certainly got attached to you quickly."

"I think he just wants to make sure I'm okay. He definitely doesn't want to get back together."

"Why would you not be okay?" Joseph's tone was thoughtful. He seemed to realize that by okay, I didn't just mean that I'd gotten over the break-up and moved on.

"In case any of the people he'd caused trouble for came after me," I said. "They have no reason to, but I guess he's a little overprotective."

"That's not necessarily a bad thing. It's good to have someone concerned with your welfare."

I didn't answer. In an effort to get away from talk of Maxwell, I said, "How about you? Do you have a girlfriend?"

"My job is my girlfriend. I travel around too much to have anyone steady."

"That must be tough."

"It was a conscious decision. I care deeply about my work, but it's a lonely profession. I knew that going in."

The growing sound of waves announced the end of the trail. The beach that opened up before us looked like something from a post-apocalyptic movie. There were two cabins still standing, as Joseph had told us, but the remains of half a dozen more were scattered along the sand. Palm trees had grown up amidst fallen rafters, and in the beam of my flashlight, I saw dried seaweed, driftwood, and even a life preserver among the ruins. It looked eerie in the moonlight.

We moved forward cautiously. I swept my flashlight across the front of the first intact cabin we came to, and I gasped when a face appeared in one of the broken windows.

Joseph followed the beam of my flashlight with his eyes. "Good spotting, Betty," he said. "You stay here and keep your light shining inside the window. I'll go in and rope him."

It turned out to be Redneck that we had caught. Joseph had no problems getting him roped, but easing Redneck down the stairs onto the beach took a while. The walk back to the barn was slow going. Joseph kept Redneck in front of us, and we chatted while we walked. I could tell by the way he talked about his job that Joseph had a real passion for history and restoring places. He had a steady supply of stories about the historic sites he had helped preserve.

"I'm a history fan, too," I admitted. "I do all of the research into a haunted site for my team. I'm the only one who really enjoys it."

"I figured you had an appreciation for days gone by," Joseph said. "You seemed most interested when I told the history of Serenity Island." He smiled at me, and even though my flashlight was pointed at the ground in front of me, I could perfectly picture those faded green eyes. Our stroll would have been pleasant if we weren't herding a revenant in front of us.

Joseph got Redneck reinstalled in the barn, and he reported that Beard had been returned, too. That left just Nosy who was still AWOL.

Joseph and I headed back to the cabins to continue our search, and this time, the walk took on a very different feel. I was a lot less cautious now that I'd grown used to the dark trees pressing in around us, and knowing that only one revenant was on the loose made me drop my guard.

Joseph walked close by my side, his arm sometimes brushing against mine. He was wearing a sweatshirt so I couldn't see his muscles, but I could smell his musky cologne. He guided our conversation to other topics, wanting to know my favorite movies, what I did for a living, and what my plans were for Christmas. It felt very much like a date, and I tried to enjoy it. Still, I kept mentally comparing Joseph to Maxwell.

We made a thorough sweep of the cabins but found no one. The beach was empty, as well. "I should have thought to get the radios before we came out," Joseph said sheepishly. "We could have saved ourselves this extra trip if the others have already found our last runaway."

"I don't mind." Because I'm supposed to be moving on with my life, I added silently, and I may as well do it with someone as handsome as you.

We took our time going back to the barn. We weren't moving quite as slowly as we had when Redneck had been with us, but we were definitely lingering. Carter and Rob weren't at the barn, and Nosy was still missing. We headed back to the lodge, continuing our leisurely pace and our friendly chatter. Was I really beginning to fall for Joseph Stryker?

Carter and Rob were just walking up from the beach

when we got to the lodge. "I wondered what happened to you," Carter said. We filled them in on our recovery of Redneck and our second, futile search.

"That leaves Nosy, then. There are a few more trails off the beach that we haven't checked yet," Rob said.

Joseph offered our services to help with the search, but Rob waved him off. "No need. We can manage it. You two get back to bed."

I had gotten my second wind and doubted that I'd be able to fall asleep quickly, but my shoulders were still sore from the grave digging, so at least I could rest my tired muscles. I rubbed my right shoulder absently as we walked up the stairs to our rooms.

"I could work on that for you if you want," Joseph said.

That sounded nice but a little too forward. "It's fine. Just a bit sore from putting Lady Gray to rest."

"Let me know if you change your mind. Good night, Betty."

"Good night, Joseph. See you in the morning." I doubted I'd have to wait very long, considering how much time our excursion had taken.

I heard Joseph's door click behind me. I was opening my own door when a hand pressed against my back.

Joseph, apparently, was hoping I had already changed my mind. I closed my eyes briefly, debating telling him to cool it or inviting him in and letting things happen as they might.

I need to tell him to back off a bit, I thought. A little flirting during our walk was one thing, but being alone with him in my bedroom was something else entirely.

I turned around, my mouth open to politely reprimand him, and the now-familiar scent reached me. I swung my flashlight up and found myself staring into Nosy's dead eyes.

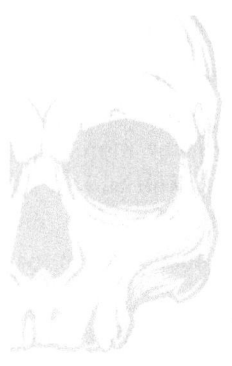

NINE

I jumped backwards by instinct, landing against the door. It yawned wide under my weight and sent me sprawling to the floor. My grip tightened on my flashlight as Nosy took a step toward me. It wasn't much of a weapon, but it was better than nothing.

"Help!" I screamed. "Joseph!"

Nosy took another step forward, his arm reaching down toward me. A low moan burbled from his mouth.

I scrambled to my feet and backed into my room, watching as Nosy stepped slowly over the threshold. It was like watching a horror movie in slow motion. Even though Nosy was too slow to corner me, I still felt threatened. I guess it's a gut instinct when a reanimated corpse is trying to grab you.

"Joseph!" I called again.

Nosy stopped moving forward, though his legs still made walking motions. Joseph was behind Nosy, holding him by the shirt.

I let out a lungful of air. "About time," I said. "Thanks."

"Grab the blanket off your bed."

I complied, passing it to Joseph as best I could without getting too close to Nosy. Joseph folded it into one long, narrow length, then deftly looped it around Nosy's waist. "We can lead him back to the barn this way," he explained.

I let Joseph lead the way out of the lodge, but as soon as we were on the trail, Nosy stopped and turned toward me. Joseph tugged on the ends of the blanket. "This way, Nosy."

Nosy leaned forward toward me, putting his weight against the blanket. The harder Joseph tugged, the further Nosy leaned away from him. It was a strange tug of war. I decided I would feel more comfortable with Joseph between me and Nosy, so I gave the two a wide berth as I passed them. Now that I was in the lead, Nosy turned to the front again and dutifully began to walk.

Nosy was following me. I wasn't sure why or how he could even discern me from anyone else on the island. As we walked to the barn, I mulled over a few possibilities for Nosy's interest in me. I quickly dismissed the possibility that he was coming after me to eat my brains. That left two options which were much more likely. One was that Nosy simply liked me. Ghosts usually retain their personalities after death, so it's inevitable that they will like some of the people who come into contact with them and dislike others. There were a lot of stories about haunted houses where the resident ghost caused nothing but trouble for the living residents. The people would move out in a hurry, swearing that the house was inhabited by an evil, spiteful spirit. The next family to take up residence, though, would experience nothing but a few footsteps or the occasional cold spot. Living happily with a ghost was a matter of finding personalities that were complementary. It was no different than finding the right roommate.

The notion that Nosy had taken a liking to me was plausible, but I thought my third option was the most likely. Nosy knew that Carter and I were there to help him, and he was anxious to communicate. He hadn't come after me tonight to attack me, but to talk to me.

At the entrance to the barn, I stopped and turned to Nosy. I spoke firmly, telling him, "I know you want to talk to me. Tomorrow morning, I promise, I will come here, and we can talk. I want to know what you're trying to tell me."

I think the message got through. Nosy stood still while Joseph unlocked the barn, and he walked in of his own accord.

Joseph tossed the blanket into the barn, too. It's not like I was ever going to put it back on my bed.

"You made a friend," Joseph said lightly on our walk back to the lodge.

"And hopefully, he'll talk to us tomorrow so we can get him to cross over." I didn't add that I was desperately hoping to get more details about the demon that had killed Nosy.

Rob and Carter were anxiously waiting for us on the front steps. "I thought you went back to your rooms, but when we got upstairs, Betty's door was open." Rob didn't sound worried, but at least Carter looked concerned.

I briefly relayed my encounter with Nosy, and Carter looked as interested as me in another EVP session in the morning. He looked at me significantly. "Maybe this time he'll give us some detailed answers," he said.

"Let's hope."

Joseph insisted on checking my room before we all went back to bed. I'm not sure why since all four of the remaining revenants were accounted for, but at least he knew that an old quilt was stashed in the trunk under my window.

"Are you okay?" Joseph asked. He put his hand lightly on my shoulder and looked at me intently.

"I'm fine. He didn't hurt me."

"I know, but I want to make sure your nerves aren't shot by what just happened. Are you comfortable sleeping alone?"

That was even more forward than Joseph's offer of a shoulder rub.

"I'm fine," I repeated. "I'll lock my door."

"All right. If you need anything, you know where to find me." Joseph leaned in and wrapped his arms around me in a tight hug. Gosh, he smelled nice. Without thinking, I slid my arms around his waist. I could feel the muscles of his back, even through his sweatshirt.

I sighed. My second wind had long since given out, and I was exhausted. Hopefully Adrienne would let us sleep a little late in the morning. I let my head sink until my forehead rested on Joseph's shoulder.

"I was really worried when I heard you scream my name." Joseph's mouth was right next to my ear, and his low voice made me shiver. He gave me a squeeze and released me. "Good night, again."

"Good night. Thank you for your help."

Joseph just smiled.

As I had hoped, Adrienne didn't wake us up until later in the morning. I still had no idea what time it was, but by the angle of the sun streaming into my room, I knew we had all gotten a couple of extra hours.

I didn't feel refreshed, though. I yawned constantly during breakfast, despite a whopping three cups of coffee. That was a lot of coffee, even for me. Joseph found my weariness amusing.

"Did you have trouble sleeping last night?" he asked. "Perhaps you didn't like being left alone after what you went through."

I saw Carter stiffen out of the corner of my eye. Clearly, I wasn't being over-imaginative in thinking that Joseph's concern had underlying implications. "I slept soundly, but I think it might take a couple of nights to get caught up. Then again, I might settle for a nice long nap this afternoon."

Our morning was half gone already, so we decided to concentrate our efforts solely on Nosy. During his EVP session, Carter and I both asked every question we could think of, except the one we really wanted to ask: "Who was the demon that killed you?" It was on the tip of my tongue the entire morning.

We had dismissed Joseph and Rob, telling them that Nosy wasn't in danger of wandering off since he actually wanted to communicate with us. That left Dwayne and Mick, and after a solid hour of EVP work, Carter politely asked them if we could have a few moments alone with Nosy.

"He found Betty when she was alone last night," Carter reasoned with them. "I think he might be more responsive if there are less people around."

Dwayne shrugged. "Okay, but leave your mics on. We'll film from a distance. Maybe we can get some good VO material."

"VO?" I asked.

"Voiceover. If we pick up any interesting clips from you two, we can play them while showing shots of the island or close-ups of the zombie."

Carter pursed his lips. As much as he craved attention, even he was frustrated that we couldn't get a break for even a few moments. He gave a curt nod, and Dwayne and Mick retreated to the edge of the clearing. Mick kept his camera trained on us, not for the visual, but for the audio.

I turned my tape recorder on and raised my eyebrows at Carter. He inclined his head slightly. We didn't need to speak to each other; we simultaneously reached back and turned off our microphones.

"What was the name of the demon who killed you?" I

asked.

After a pause, during which I hoped Nosy had answered us, I added, "You said 'they' couldn't help you. Who are 'they'?"

"Why did a demon want to kill you?" Carter chimed in.

"Hey!" Dwayne shouted. I turned and saw him trotting toward us. "Both of your mics went out at the same time. We should still be in range to pick them up, so I'm not sure what's going on."

We turned to face Dwayne, and I knew Carter was quickly turning his mic back on, just as I was. "You're not hearing us anymore?" he asked innocently.

"No, it just went silent. Let me see." Dwayne checked both of our battery packs. "Full power," he mumbled.

I pointed at Mick. "I think he's trying to say something to you."

Dwayne turned and saw that Mick was waving his arm, giving a thumbs up. "Hmm, we're back in business, I guess. That was weird."

"Dealing with the paranormal can cause all kinds of strange electrical phenomena," I said. Carter choked down a laugh.

We asked more questions before breaking for lunch. We were going to have a very boring afternoon of going over such a long EVP session. After the night's drama, though, I was perfectly ready for some boredom.

When Carter found the first EVP from Nosy, he had to wake me up to listen. I had just planned to close my eyes for a few minutes. Carter's window was cracked open, and the sound of the waves had lulled me to sleep.

I sat up, covering a yawn with one hand, and patting

my hair into place with the other. "Whatcha got?" I mumbled.

"Nosy was definitely ready to talk. We got a response to the first question. Listen."

My voice blared through the headphones. "What do you want to tell us?"

"Afraid," was Nosy's distinct reply.

I bit my lip. "He probably knows he's dead," I began.

"And maybe he's afraid to cross over," Carter finished for me.

"Maybe Nosy will be easy to take care of, like Lady Gray. Great catch, Carter." I lay back down and relaxed while Carter continued his search.

Nosy had clammed up after that first answer, until we had turned off our mics. By then, I was listening to the audio while Carter snoozed. There was no response to my first question, asking what demon had been responsible for Nosy's death. The second question, regarding the mysterious "they" who couldn't save him, yielded a "hhhhh" noise. It sounded like Nosy had serious respiratory problems rather than an actual word.

With such a slow start, I wasn't expecting an answer to "Why did the demon kill you?" I got one, but it made no sense to me. It sounded like a really long word, but for the life of me I couldn't make it out. After five attempts at interpreting it, I gave up and woke Carter with a jab to his leg.

"Don't hit me," he said, instantly awake.

"I'm mystified by this one," I told him. "Let's see if you can figure it out."

Carter listened. He frowned. Then he listened again. As he played the same clip over and over again, he began to move his lips along with Nosy's voice. Soon, he was sounding it out. "Killer be kilt," he repeated. "Kill or be killed."

I sucked in my breath. "Nosy died fighting the demon?" Being killed by a demon was one thing; fighting back was another.

Nosy had been a demon hunter. When I proposed my theory to Carter, he raised a warning finger. "Not necessarily. Plenty of ordinary people have fought demons. Look at you: you banished one, and you're definitely not a hunter. Demonologists battle demons."

"But not in physical form," I argued.

"Nosy could be speaking about a spiritual battle. You associate demons with flesh and blood now because of your experiences, but they are much more likely to be spiritual entities."

Carter was right. I was jumping to wild conclusions. I guess I'd seen too much of demon hunters lately.

"This means we have a whole new slew of questions to ask Nosy," I said.

"And we need to ask them when no one else is around."

"Agreed."

There was a knock on Carter's door, and I jumped. Carter laughed at me. "Zombies don't knock, you know."

"Ha, ha."

Of course it wasn't a zombie at the door. It was Joseph. "How's it going?" he asked hopefully.

"We think Nosy died in a fight," Carter said. "Maybe he got into an argument with someone, and it turned violent."

"You're making some progress. Congratulations. I actually came up to see if either of you need anything from the mainland. Adrienne and Rob are going to take the boat in to pick up some new survey equipment that should have arrived yesterday."

"I could use some hot water," I answered. We really didn't want for anything else. Even with our primitive quarters, I could see why people were willing to pay handsomely to vacation at Serenity Island. It took me a moment to realize that it was Monday. Instead of working away behind my cluttered desk in my tiny office, I was lounging on a bed and listening to the sound of waves.

"I'm going to go for a walk on the beach," I decided. The only time I'd gotten out on the sand was during last night's search for the revenants, and that didn't count. I needed to feel the sunshine on my face and the sand between my toes. It wasn't warm out, but it wasn't too cold. I could get away with a little bit of barefoot time.

"Carter?" I prompted.

"Nah. I'm good right here."

Joseph offered to walk me downstairs, and I wasn't surprised when he asked if I wanted company. I readily agreed.

It was a beautiful day. Only a few clouds streaked the blue sky, and the low tide gave us plenty of white sand to walk over. I carried my shoes in one hand, enjoying the squish of the damp sand underfoot.

"There's something out here that a history lover like you can appreciate," Joseph told me. "It's down near the south end of the island."

The island hadn't looked that big when we had arrived on the boat, but walking down the eastern beach was a longer hike than I anticipated. The trees behind us hid the lodge and the dock, and it felt like Joseph and I had the island to ourselves.

Joseph was again walking close to my side, and his fingers brushed against mine a few times. We rounded a cluster of palm trees, and Joseph stopped. "There," he said, pointing.

A mass of gray steel rose up out of the water. It was covered with rust and had huge gaping holes, but still I recognized it as a military ship. The white numbers on its hull had dulled to a shade of gray that was only barely discernible from the steel on which they were painted.

"That's amazing." I wasn't saying it to be polite.

"Come on, we'll take a closer look." This time, when Joseph's fingers met mine, he took my hand and pulled me forward.

The ship sat half submerged in the water, and Joseph explained that this was the most we would be able to see since it was low tide.

"How did it wind up here?" I asked.

"Did you know that German U-boats made it all the way to the East Coast during World War II? Ships like this patrolled the coast, hoping to intercept them. A hurricane proved more dangerous than a German sub for this ship."

"How many of the men died?"

"None. A larger vessel that could withstand the waves rescued the crew. When Serenity Island Resort was open, the crew would have reunions here every few years. They would all troop out here and relive that storm."

Joseph paused and stole a glance at me, his eyes bright. "You were wondering if it was haunted, weren't you?"

"Of course. If you'd said that men had died on this ship, I'd probably be back out here tonight with my tape recorder and my camera."

"Well, don't let the lack of ghosts keep you from a nighttime walk out here. I'd be happy to bring you back after dinner. The ship does look spooky in the moonlight."

I nodded my head vaguely, too absorbed by the vision of the ship. Its hull now towered over us, and I put one hand against the huge links of the anchor chain.

"Watch your step," Joseph warned.

Debris from the wreck was nearly buried by years of shifting sand, but bits of rusted metal poked out of the ground in places. I put my shoes back on and tried to keep my eyes on the ground as I moved forward.

"Is it safe to go onboard?" I asked. I was already calculating how high of a boost Joseph would have to give me so I could reach a short ladder welded to the starboard side of the bow.

"No, it's too dangerous. I understand there's nothing to see inside, anyway. The men who served on her took all the souvenirs they could during their reunions. Anything that's left is either rusted or rotted."

Darn.

"Come look at what's on the other side." Again, Joseph took my hand and led me around the front of the bow. The angle of the ship and the direction of the waves had created a shallow pool, and crabs and a few small fish were happily going about their business within. "High tide covers the pool completely, but there are always some creatures left here when the tide goes out."

We lingered for a while, watching the crabs scuttling over the sand. Joseph, I noted, still had my hand firmly in his. Our walk back to the lodge was just as pleasant, and I hoped very much that I'd get that nighttime walk after dinner.

I got my wish. We all lingered over dinner, and it was late before we broke up for the evening. I began to follow Carter upstairs, but Joseph called my name softly and motioned me to follow him out the front doors. As I turned toward him, I briefly saw the frown that creased Carter's face. Was he jealous?

Surely not, I told myself. I was just letting Daisy's wild fears get the best of my imagination.

It was a windy night, and the waves crashing on the shore sounded angry. The tide was coming in, and the beach had shrunk significantly. I kept my shoes on this time, not wanting to step on anything in the dark.

Joseph tried making conversation, but the wind was so ¹ud that we practically had to shout at each other. He soon gave up, and we walked silently but contentedly. Our pace was slow, and instead of taking my hand this time, Joseph wrapped his arm lightly around my waist.

The shipwreck was every bit as spooky as Joseph had promised. The hull seemed to glow in the moonlight, and even though it wasn't haunted, it sure looked like it should be. I stopped when we got closer, admiring the perfect picture that the ship, the moon, and the palm trees presented. It was like something out of a painting and hardly seemed real.

"It takes on a different life in the darkness, doesn't it?" Joseph was leaning down to speak close to my ear, and the resonance of his voice made me shiver. He mistook it as a reaction to the cool air and wrapped his arms around me. I was reminded again of the difference between Maxwell's hot skin and Joseph's normal, human temperature.

Don't think about Maxwell, I told myself. You aren't trying to replace him; you're trying to move on.

I concentrated on Joseph's muscular arms holding me tight against his firm chest and on the way his fingers gently traced circles against my back.

And then I was concentrating on the way Joseph's lips felt against mine. He kissed me deeply, one hand coming up to cradle my head as he pulled me closer. The blonde stubble on his cheeks prickled against my skin, but his lips were soft, even though the kiss was not.

I was definitely not thinking about Maxwell now.

Joseph deepened his kiss, and I felt his tongue pushing impatiently against my lips. I obliged just as his fingers entwined with my hair, tugging hard enough that I whimpered. My reaction only spurred Joseph further. He pulled steadily on my hair, forcing my head back so he could kiss his way down my neck. There was no finesse in Joseph's actions, just raw passion and absolute confidence that he was going to get what he wanted.

And I knew exactly what he wanted a moment later, when his hips angled forward, and I could feel his hardness pressing against me. I gasped and pulled back as much as I could. Kissing Joseph was wonderful, but I wasn't prepared to do any more than that. Joseph seemed to understand why I was hesitant, but his smile was conspiratorial as he loosened his grip to give me a few inches of breathing room. He was clearly a man who could handle a setback without giving up the fight. When he kissed me again, it was gentler, though I could feel his restraint.

We stayed there on the beach until I really did begin to shiver from the cold. It had been a while since I'd had an honest-to-goodness make-out session with a guy. I would have been happy to stay right there with Joseph, but the chill put a damper on my pleasure.

Joseph kept one arm around my shoulders as we walked back to the lodge. Instead of a sauntering, romantic stroll, I moved as briskly as I could over the sand. The vision of a roaring fire in my room's fireplace made me anxious for the indoors. As we walked, I glanced at Joseph occasionally, confused about my feelings for him. I liked him, but a part of me felt like I was betraying Maxwell. I had been telling myself that I needed to move on, but maybe I wasn't ready to dive into anything new. My memories of Maxwell were still too fresh, and after all he'd done for me, I had nothing bad to make me regret my time with him. Yes, he'd broken up with me, but it was for my own safety. I was sure Maxwell wasn't out kissing some new woman right now, so how could I even think about kissing Joseph?

I glanced at Joseph again. He was looking toward the ocean, his eyes squinting against the wind and his profile outlined perfectly in the moonlight. If I wait until I feel ready to move on, I realized, I'll never actually do it. I just have to take the plunge. I shut my eyes briefly and took a deep breath. Relax, I told myself, and stop analyzing everything.

The lodge was silent when we returned, and all of the lights were off downstairs. Neither of us had thought to bring a flashlight, so we crept carefully up the stairs. I wasn't uncomfortable with the darkness until I remembered Nosy's late-night visit. When Joseph insisted on walking me all the way to my door, I welcomed the company.

I should have known that Joseph would want to do more than see me to the door. I stepped over the threshold and turned to wish him a good night, but before I could get any words out, he caught me in a crushing embrace and began kissing me again. That eagerness I had sensed from him before had returned, and I felt myself unconsciously stepping backwards.

It was to no avail. Joseph lifted me effortlessly from the ground and carried me across the room without ever breaking our kiss. He roughly laid me down on the bed and pinned me there with his body.

I had been kissing him back, though my passion wasn't equal to his. This, though, was too much. Kissing on the sand was one thing; kissing me in my bed was another.

It took effort to break our kiss, and I sucked in a lungful of air. "Joseph, please," I said.

He took it as a very different kind of please.

"I can't do this," I said, my voice firmer.

Joseph sighed loudly, in between nibbles on my ear. "Please don't make me stop."

"I have to." I would have pulled away from him if I wasn't stuck between his body and the bed.

"Why?"

Now it was my turn to sigh. "I don't even know you that well. We just met," I did the math, "three days ago."

"I don't care."

"I do. Joseph, I can't do this. Not now."

Either my persistence or my tone of voice finally persuaded him, and he rolled off me onto the bed. "Is there someone else?"

"What do you mean?"

"You say you're single, but I think you're not being honest with me. If you were, you wouldn't be sending me away. Is it Carter?"

Hadn't we been down this road before? I opened my mouth to deny anything between Carter and me, but I gave up and put my hands up defensively. "This has nothing to do with anyone else, and everything to do with me not knowing you well enough. I'm sorry. Believe me, I'm tempted, but I know I'd regret it."

Joseph stared at me, his eyes narrowed. I couldn't tell if he was angry or just carefully considering his next words. He sat up and took my hand, bringing it up to his lips. "I don't want you to have any regrets," he said softly. "But I also don't want to miss the chance of being with you."

I smiled wryly. "You're stuck here with me for another week and a half."

"I know, and I plan to make the most of it, but at a pace you're comfortable with." Joseph rose and pulled me to my feet. "I'm not giving up."

"I'm not asking you to. I just need you to slow down."

Joseph nodded reluctantly, and I followed him to the door, where I wished him a good night. I poked my head into the hallway to watch his retreat and caught sight of a form in the shadows near the stairs.

My heartbeat quickened until I realized it was just Rob. He had clearly seen Joseph coming out of my room, and he did not look happy about it.

Oh, boy. It was going to be one awkward breakfast in the morning.

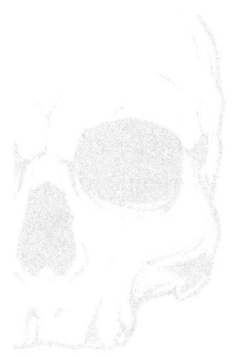

TEN

It was raining when I woke up on Tuesday. I hadn't slept well at all, and I would have much rather snuggled under the covers for another hour. Instead, I lurched out of bed and counted on the cold shower to wake me up completely.

Joseph was already in the dining room when I entered, and when he turned his eyes to me, I could feel my cheeks grow warm. Instead of being put off by my previous night's reaction to his advances, though, Joseph greeted me warmly. "Did you sleep well?" he asked, already filling a coffee cup for me.

I shook my head. "I had a hard time turning my brain off."

"I'll gladly take the blame for that." Joseph raised his cup in a mock toast and looked proud of himself.

A muffled "humph!" behind me signaled Rob's entrance. His little eyes were in danger of popping out of his skull as he looked first to Joseph, then to me. Joseph didn't seem to notice the sudden tension in the room, but I did. I tried—and failed—to smile at Rob, then gave up and sat down in my chair. I kept my eyes on my coffee.

Carter was completely oblivious to any of it. He entered cheerfully, boasting that he'd gotten the best sleep of his life.

"If you're so well-rested, then why don't you grab our mics out of the kitchen?" I suggested.

I regretted making the request as soon as I realized that it left me alone with Joseph and Rob again. Carter's face looked thoughtful when he returned. "Adrienne doesn't seem herself this morning," he said, handing me my mic.

"How so?"

"I don't know. Distracted. She usually says good morning when I go in there, and today she was just staring out the window, like she was in a daze."

"Perhaps none of the ladies slept well last night," Joseph suggested.

I shrugged when Carter raised an eyebrow at me. "I had a hard time falling asleep last night."

Rob was stoically silent as we waited for Adrienne to serve our breakfast, but Joseph and Carter chatted easily. I continued to closely examine my coffee, still too uncomfortable to chance catching Rob's eye. There was also a part of me that was terrified that Carter would find out about Joseph and me. I suspected that it wouldn't make Carter happy. It would also, I was sure, prompt a speech from him about professionalism and not dating clients.

I was relieved when Adrienne brought out our breakfast, but as she reached over to put my plate in front of me, I saw that her hand was shaking. My sausages were in danger of rolling right off onto the table.

I caught her wrist and helped guide the plate down, then turned to her. "Adrienne, what is it?"

"A ghost." Adrienne's voice was barely above a whisper.

"Where?"

"In my room, last night."

I got up and pulled an extra chair over to my side of the table. "Please, sit and tell us what happened."

Adrienne looked unsure about being the center of

attention, but she sat dutifully. Out of the corner of my eye, I saw Dwayne lean in with his camera. "And speak loudly," he instructed.

"There isn't much to tell. I woke up last night, and I just felt like I wasn't alone. I could see the outline of someone standing in front of my window. He just stood there and didn't move. I thought one of you had somehow gotten in my room. I keep a flashlight on the nightstand, so I grabbed it and turned it on. When I did, nobody was there."

"Did you go back to sleep after that?" Carter asked.

"No. I lit all my oil lamps and tried to go back to sleep, hoping the light would keep the ghost away. When I closed my eyes, though, I started hearing noises."

"What kind of noises?" I prompted.

Adrienne brought her palm down hard against the table. "Pounding, like this. It sounded like someone stomping down the hallway, but it paused every few seconds. It sounded like he was stopping at every door to listen."

"Did you go out in the hallway to look?" Carter asked.

Adrienne shook her head, recoiling at the thought of facing the entity.

"Did you get any sense of what the ghost looked like?" he continued.

"It was a man. I could just tell, you know? There were no details, but he looked tall."

"How did he make you feel?" I asked.

"Terrified, of course! I woke up to find a ghost in my bedroom. How would you feel?"

"Well, yes, you had every right to be startled," I said. "What I meant was, did the ghost give you the impression that he wanted to cause you any harm? Did you feel like you were in danger?"

Adrienne was quiet for a few moments. "Yes," she

finally said. "He scared the living daylights out of me, and I hate to think what would have happened if I hadn't woken up."

I turned to Carter and smiled, despite Adrienne's concern. Having an ordinary haunting to investigate would be a nice respite from the revenants. There was no chance that a ghost was going to literally spill his guts right in front of me.

Carter and I offered reassurances to Adrienne, who looked a little more confident when she stood and returned to the kitchen. As soon as she disappeared through the door, Joseph laughed. "Betty, you look downright eager to track down this ghost."

"Since it's raining out, we may as well stay indoors and do a little investigating," I said. "EVP sessions with the revenants won't do us any good today; there will be too much noise from the rain if we try to conduct them outdoors. And I'm guessing that none of us wants to go inside the barn to work with them."

Everyone agreed, and Carter looked eager, too. Even he seemed glad to be back in his paranormal comfort zone.

Adrienne was nice enough to let us start our investigation in her room after breakfast. Joseph and Rob declined the chance to sit in there with us, which gave me a great deal of relief, but Joseph promised to be close by in case we needed him. He and Rob both denied any knowledge of deaths at the lodge, but over its long history, it was likely that a guest or two had passed on while vacationing.

Rob was still glaring at me as Carter and I headed upstairs. Rob had been harmless enough during our stay, but I was beginning to dislike him. Something about the way he was looking at me made my skin crawl, and I wondered why I hadn't felt that way earlier.

Because, I answered myself, he wasn't looking at me that way earlier.

I turned my back on his stare and continued upstairs. Carter and I got our equipment and went into Adrienne's room, which, unsurprisingly, was in perfect order. Her personal things were neatly arranged on top of an antique vanity, and the bed was made with precision. Mick followed us in with his camera, and it was really hard to act like he wasn't there when the three of us were in such a small space together.

"She said the ghost was over here, in front of the window," Carter said, looking at the floor as if it might show telltale footprints.

"What if it was someone outside the window?" I asked. "It could have been Rob or Joseph walking on the balcony."

"If that's the case, then why didn't one of them speak up about it?"

"Yeah, good point."

"You said you didn't sleep well, Betty. Did you hear any stomping in the hallway?"

"Not a peep. It was perfectly quiet."

"Well, let's get started. It feels odd, doesn't it? I'm not used to doing this stuff in the daylight." Carter settled onto the bed, his tape recorder already in his hand.

We conducted an EVP session, checked temperature readings with Carter's digital gauge, and took some photos. It was utterly boring. The only thing we achieved was that we noticed the temperature was slowly dropping in Adrienne's room. There was nothing paranormal about it, though: the rain was sweeping through Georgia with a cold front hard on its heels.

Carter and I looked at each other. "We're not getting anything," he said.

"Nope."

"Let's try again tonight. We'll talk Adrienne into

coming with us. Maybe the ghost particularly wanted to see her."

"Maybe."

Mick looked thoroughly disappointed in our lackluster investigation. He made us each sit and give a brief interview, and I explained that frequent investigating helps you hone your intuition, and you get better at sensing when something paranormal is about to happen. Carter and I were feeling absolutely nothing.

I suddenly felt a little sorry for both Mick and Dwayne. If it was boring for us, then it must be doubly so for them, stuck behind their cameras. "What do you believe?" I suddenly asked Mick. "Do you even believe in ghosts, or do you think Carter and I are a couple of nuts?"

Mick lowered his camera and looked at me thoughtfully. "They're real, all right. And there are worse things out there than ghosts. Worse than these zombies, even."

"You've got that right," I agreed. Maxwell had once said the same thing to me.

Carter and I probably should have gone straight to his room to begin going over evidence, but we both wanted a break. Instead, we went down to the lobby and started rummaging through a bookcase next to the massive fireplace. The books were all mildewed, but Carter let out a shout of triumph when he pulled a chess set from the bottom shelf. It was filthy with dust and grime, so we grabbed rags from the kitchen and set to work cleaning each piece. Even Mick pitched in after filming us for a few minutes. "It's not like we need footage of you two cleaning house," he said.

Once the chess set was gleaming, we set it up in the dining room and set about trying to defeat each other. Carter was a lot better than me, and he gloated every time he won.

I was on the brink of winning when Joseph and Rob

came in looking for lunch. "Oh, we'll clear this out of the way," Carter said, sweeping away the chess pieces with one arm.

"You little—" I began, until I caught sight of Mick's camera. "I was about to win," I said instead. Being pouty wouldn't look good on camera, but it was probably a step above swearing at Carter.

"You didn't win fast enough," Carter answered.

Adrienne was back to her usual efficiency when she served lunch, though she was hesitant to join us in investigating her room that night. "I don't want to see the ghost again," she said.

"We'll be with you the whole time," Carter assured her. "And if we can talk to him, then we can ask him to please leave you alone."

That did the trick for Adrienne, and we agreed we'd start right after dinner that night.

The time between lunch and dinner absolutely dragged by. Carter and I reviewed the morning's EVP session to no avail, which was no surprise. We played some more chess, I paced through the lobby until the dust made me sneeze constantly, and I laid in bed for a while, just listening to the waves and the rain.

My only respite came late in the afternoon when Joseph knocked on my door. I let him in, hoping he wasn't going to repeat last night's performance. He took me by the waist and pulled me to him. "I think there's a ghost in my room," he said. "Can you come investigate there later tonight?" Joseph's lips were already pressing against my earlobe as he spoke.

"I doubt your partner would approve."

Joseph pulled back and looked at me, surprised. "Rob? What do you mean?"

I explained that I'd seen him in the hallway the night before and that he'd been looking very unhappy with me all day. "Didn't you notice how tense it was during breakfast?" I concluded.

"I was only paying attention to you," Joseph said. Fully recovered from his initial surprise, he took my face in his hands and stroked my jawline with his thumbs. He leaned in and kissed me. I stepped back, uncertain about his unrelenting advances, but Joseph petulantly pulled me closer. Before he could kiss me again, a loud bang sounded in the hallway. It sounded like someone had dropped a bowling ball.

I flinched and released Joseph, moving toward the door to find out what had made the noise. My thoughts instantly turned to Adrienne's claims of a ghost stomping up and down the hallway. Joseph was right behind me, neither of us thinking about the fact that we might raise suspicion when we both emerged from my room.

Carter was the only one in the hallway, his back to us. As we watched, he jumped and landed hard on the wooden floor, making the same booming noise we'd just heard. Then he began to walk, taking big strides and bringing his feet down hard with each step.

I giggled. He looked so ridiculous striding down the hall like that.

Carter turned around when he heard me, his face reddening. "I thought I'd try to recreate the sounds that Adrienne heard," he said. At that moment, she came running out of her room. "Yes, that's it," she said. "Not the first big sound, but the quieter ones."

"These," Carter said, and he took a few more big strides. I giggled again.

"Yes, yes, those. But why would a ghost go stomping down the hallway? I thought they didn't usually make noises."

Carter stopped walking and quickly recovered his usual

demeanor. "He might want attention. Maybe he wants to tell us something or is just lonely."

Adrienne nodded. "Maybe. I hope we can help him tonight."

"That's the spirit," Carter said. Without looking at us again, he followed Adrienne back into her room and shut the door.

"Well," I said after a moment.

"Good for him," Joseph said approvingly, his implication clear.

Joseph moved to return to my room, but I put a hand on his chest to stop him. "I think I want to rest for a while," I said.

"You certainly like to torture me. Patience is not my virtue," Joseph said, but he returned to his own room after giving me a brief kiss.

I watched Carter and Adrienne keenly during our investigation in her room that night. I wasn't jealous, but I was curious to see if there were any signs that Carter was doing more than just helping her with her haunting.

The three of us were sitting on the floor in front of the fireplace with Dwayne and Mick both filming us. It was really crowded in that room. Adrienne had built up a fire in all of our rooms to combat the steadily dropping temperature outside, so when Carter called for lights out, we weren't even close to being in the dark. As soon as I blew out the two oil lamps, though, Adrienne's hand found Carter's and clamped tight. I looked at Carter and raised my eyebrows. He shrugged and gave me a lopsided smile, as if to say, "I don't know, either."

Like our investigation earlier that afternoon, things were fairly quiet. Carter had just asked the ghost to give us a sign of his presence when a loud bang sounded from the window. We all jumped, and Carter hurried to the balcony door to look outside. A cold gust of air rushed in as he opened it, and I crossed my arms against the chill.

Carter looked perplexed when he came back inside. "It was a seagull," he said, sitting down. "It looks like he flew right into the window and got a little dazed. He flew off when I went out there."

"So either our ghost was giving us a sign, or it was incredible timing on the part of the seagull," I said.

"It was a sign," Adrienne said, her eyes wide. Her fingers searched for Carter's again.

"We don't know that for sure," I said, at the same time that Carter said, "I think you're right."

I considered telling Carter to cut out the dramatics but decided to let the cameras catch what they might.

"Carter, go back outside," I said suddenly. He looked at me like he was slightly offended. "I'm not trying to kick you out," I explained. "I want you to stand in front of the window so we can test the theory that Adrienne's ghost was really just someone on the balcony."

Carter did as I instructed, but we couldn't see his shadow outside the window. The fireplace was too bright in contrast with the darkness outside.

"Okay, so that theory can be crossed off the list," I said.

We spent the rest of our time there asking the ghost to please leave Adrienne alone and to not show up in her room anymore. "If you are trying to communicate with us," Carter said, "then you're welcome to come to my room or to Betty's. We want to know what you have to say."

"Gee, thanks for volunteering me," I muttered. I was fine with encountering ghosts during an investigation, and I was perfectly comfortable with Lieutenant Griffin at home, but I wasn't comfortable with a strange ghost waking me up in the middle of the night for a heart-to-heart chat. Once Carter was on a roll, though, there was no stopping him.

"Betty, keep your camera and your tape recorder next to you tonight, just in case," he said. I reluctantly agreed, and then we decided to call it a night. It was getting late, and Adrienne had to get up earlier than the rest of us to get breakfast ready. Despite her initial fear, she was now yawning and casting longing looks at her bed.

The hallway was quiet when we emerged from Adrienne's room, and I guessed that Joseph and Rob were already in their rooms for the night. I said good night while Carter promised Adrienne that he'd be at her side in a heartbeat if she got scared. He was so focused on her that he completely forgot to wish me a good night.

The fire had warmed my room considerably, and I stacked the two logs Adrienne had left for me on top of it. After sleeping so badly the night before, I expected to drop off to sleep instantly. Instead, I lay there, staring at the leaping shadows on the ceiling and wondering if the ghost would actually try to communicate with me during the night. As Carter had requested, my camera and tape recorder were on my nightstand, just in case. The idea of an unfamiliar ghost coming to see me while I was sleeping made me miss Lieutenant Griffin. Thinking of him made me realize how much I missed my cat and my apartment, too, and soon I was desperately wishing I had a cell phone signal so I could call Daisy. I had only been on Serenity Island for four days, but the absolute isolation from the rest of the world made me feel like I'd been gone from home for weeks.

I was too restless to stay in bed, so I pulled my jacket on over my pajamas and went out onto the balcony. The rain had slowed to a soft drizzle, and fog was gathering along the trail to the dock. The clouds had obscured the stars, and the only light I saw was from a ship miles off the coast.

As I watched, a light flared below me. I squinted in an effort to see through the darkness, but all I could make out was a dim point of light. A flashlight. I watched its beam sweep forward along the trail as whoever was holding it moved toward the beach.

We had left Adrienne's room at ten o'clock, and I'd been trying to fall asleep for at least an hour. Who could possibly want to go to the beach at this time, in this weather?

Curiosity got the better of me. In no time, I got dressed, putting on both my sweatshirt and my jacket since just standing on the balcony for a few minutes had given me a chill. I opened my door and crept as quietly as I could down the hallway. I considered inviting Carter to join me. When I raised my hand to his door, though, I heard a soft giggle coming from his room. I lowered my hand and kept walking, making my way down the dark stairs with a hand clamped firmly on the railing.

When I was outside, I sprinted across the trail toward the dock. I arrived at the beach with no idea where to go. I didn't know if the person I'd seen had gone straight, onto the dock, or right, down the beach. The fog was closing in around me, and I didn't have a flashlight of my own.

I gazed down the beach and was rewarded with the briefest flicker of light. I took off that way, slowing as I got near the area where I guessed the flash of light had come from. I didn't want to accidentally walk right into whomever I was following.

As the distance grew, I despaired of ever seeing the flashlight's beam again. Its owner must have struck off down some path through the trees that led to the middle of the island. I turned and faced the tree line, holding my breath and listening hard. Over the sound of the waves behind me, I heard the snap of a twig. A footstep?

It was followed by several crunching noises, which I recognized as someone walking over fallen palm fronds. They were soft, slow footsteps, and they were heading right for me.

I expected to see Rob or Joseph emerge from the fog. Instead, I found myself face to face with a child, his dark hair tangled over his forehead and his emaciated arms rising slowly toward me.

The little boy was dead.

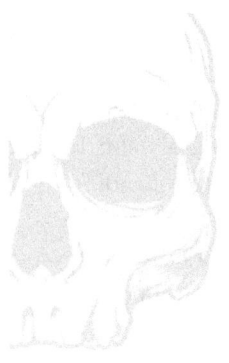

ELEVEN

I pushed my hands over my mouth to keep from screaming and backed away. The child continued to move toward me, and I felt the waves lapping at my ankles as I tried to maintain the distance between us. Where had this child come from? I had assumed that every revenant on Serenity Island had been accounted for. If this boy had been wandering through the woods, though, he might have escaped observation.

I was torn between fear and pity. He had certainly startled me, but this boy—this ghost—needed help as much as the adult revenants. Were his parents mourning the loss of their child? Did they even know he was dead?

Either way, the boy was still walking toward me, and soon we would both be in the ocean. I turned and began to walk back toward the lodge, figuring we could track the boy down in the morning. I took a few steps and stopped short. Someone was walking from the direction of the woods. The person was moving too fast to be a revenant, and I saw the beam of a flashlight moving closer to me.

I should have hailed the person and asked for help dealing with the little boy. It would have been the logical thing to do, but some part of me was immediately suspicious. A late-night walk on a cold, rainy, foggy beach was odd enough, but I suspected that they had been walking with a purpose, and that the boy was tied to it somehow. If someone was hiding the presence of another revenant from us, then it couldn't be for any good reasons. Were Dwayne and Mick doing it so they could spring the child on us in hopes of "good television"? Were Rob and Joseph trying to hide the real number of revenants for fear that we'd give up the case?

An angry rumble from the approaching person snapped me out of my thoughts. I turned, neatly sidestepped the boy, and raced down the beach as quietly as I could. I had seen something I wasn't supposed to see, of that I was certain, and I didn't want anyone to know it.

I ran until I reached the shipwreck, slipping around the far side of the bow. The tide was going out, and there was space for me to squat down on the sand, my back against the steel hull.

My ears strained to hear anything over the wind and the waves, but it was silent. The rain pelted down again in earnest, and within minutes, I was soaking wet. My clothes hung heavily on me, and I began to shiver.

I stayed there until my thighs and lower back ached from squatting. I stood slowly but was still too afraid to return to the lodge. I continued to wait. The rain eventually subsided, and I decided to take advantage of the break to begin the long walk up the beach.

I crept slowly, stopping every few feet to listen for sounds of approaching feet. It took me a long time to get back to the trail that led to the lodge, but eventually, I arrived, shivering and aching from weariness.

The fog had thickened, and I was grateful that it would help hide me from anyone who might be looking out from the lodge. I stuck close to the side of the trail, hoping the overhanging vegetation would conceal me further. There was nothing I could do to hide the wet trail I left in my wake as I returned up the stairs. If it didn't dry by morning, then it would be blatantly obvious that I'd been out during the night.

Once I was back in my room, I stripped off my wet clothes and put them in the bathtub so I wouldn't leave a puddle on the floor. I towel dried my hair vigorously and pulled on my pajamas. The fire had died down to just a few orange embers, and my room wasn't much warmer than the temperature outside.

Finally in bed, I folded my musty old quilt in half and drew my knees up to my chest. No matter how tightly I curled up, though, I couldn't stop shivering. I would have put my jacket on over my pajamas if it weren't soaking wet.

I dozed once or twice, waking up with my muscles aching from the cold. The clouds finally cleared, and moonlight filtered in through my curtains. I fell asleep again, wishing it was the warm sun shining down instead of the moon.

I woke up suddenly, my misery temporarily replaced by fear. Someone was in my room.

My eyes strained to see in the darkness, but all I could make out was the figure of a person standing at the foot of my bed. I blinked, wondering if Adrienne's ghost had come to visit me.

"Who's there?" I whispered.

In answer, the form moved slowly toward me, walking around my bed until it stood right next to me. If I had reached for my camera or tape recorder, I would have brushed against its arm.

A hand reached out and touched my shoulder, then moved to my cheek. The fingers felt hot against my freezing skin, and I gasped, realizing that this wasn't a ghost at all.

"Maxwell?"

Now that he was closer, I could see that it was the

demon leaning over me, his blue eyes almost shining in the dark room. He straightened up and began unbuttoning his shirt. After he laid it aside, he slid out of his pants, then lifted the edge of the blanket and lay in the bed next to me. Maxwell opened his arms and pulled me to him, cradling my head against his chest and stretching the length of his body against mine.

My shivering stopped, replaced by a wonderful feeling of warmth and security. I had never thought that I would be so grateful for the unnatural heat that demons radiate. Maxwell never said a word; he just stroked my hair and leaned down to kiss my forehead softly.

"Maxwell," I whispered again.

In answer, he just held me tighter. I wanted to ask him so many questions, but his warmth and my exhaustion combined to make my eyelids close against my will. I fell asleep, unafraid and happy for the first time in weeks.

I have no idea how long Maxwell stayed with me. When I awoke the next morning, he was gone. There was no sign that he had even been there, and I wondered if it hadn't been just a dream. It had felt so real, though, and I had been so warm after hours of shivering.

Reluctantly, I got out of bed and felt the sting of the cold air. I skipped taking a shower; I'd had enough of being soaking wet to last me for a while. My warmest clothes were still a dripping tangle in the bathtub, so I put on a long-sleeved shirt instead.

I slipped out of my room and knocked quietly on Carter's door. Even if Adrienne had spent the entire night with him, she would have gotten up and headed down to prepare breakfast much earlier. I was grateful for that: I didn't want any awkward scenes arising from whatever she and Carter had going on.

Carter answered the door wearing nothing but a towel around his waist. I must have looked distraught because he immediately waved me in and shut the door behind me without saying a word.

"Carter," I said quietly, putting a hand to my eyes. "Please put on some clothes."

"Are you okay?"

"I will be once you're wearing more than a towel."

Carter chuckled, but he disappeared into the bathroom and re-emerged in slacks and a sweater. "Much better," I said. He motioned me to sit on the bed, and I didn't need a prompt to begin telling him about my walk the night before.

I spoke in a quiet voice for fear that someone might overhear, and Carter leaned closer and closer to me as my story progressed. When I finished with my walk back to the lodge, Carter was silent.

"Who were you following last night, I wonder?" he asked. "It had to be either Stryker or Rob."

"Yeah, it definitely wasn't you or Adrienne," I said, trying to keep my tone casual.

Carter actually blushed. "How did you know?"

"I was going to ask if you wanted to come with me last night, so I stopped at your door. I know you don't have that girly of a giggle."

"It also could have been Mick or Dwayne," Carter said.

"Giggling in your room?"

"No, out on the beach last night." Carter playfully punched me in the arm, but he still looked embarrassed.

"Yeah, I thought of that, too. Maybe they want to surprise us with the kid and capture our reactions for the show. What should we do?"

"We keep an eye out for anything strange and be prepared to have the kid sprung on us at any moment."

"We could just ask Mick and Dwayne what they know," I suggested.

Carter shook his head. "You were right that there's something weird going on here. I think it's best if we keep this between us until we know more."

"I agree. Oh, and Carter? Can I borrow something to wear? All of my heaviest clothes got soaked last night, and it's freezing out."

Carter chose the preppiest sweater he owned to loan me. I was a little horrified by it, but at least it was cozy and warm. I just ignored the inquiring looks that Joseph and Rob gave me at breakfast.

It was hard looking at the two of them as we ate, wondering if either of them had been the one I was following. It was also tough to keep the news of Maxwell's visit to myself. I was so happy that he'd come to see me—well, if I hadn't dreamed the whole thing, I reminded myself—that I wanted to shout it out to everyone. What I really wanted to do was call Daisy and tell her. I could just picture her squeal of surprise when I told her about it.

Instead, I was mostly silent while we ate, though I did have to stifle a laugh when Adrienne put Carter's plate down in front of him. She brushed against him as she did so, giving him a suggestive smile. If she was going to be involved with Carter, then clearly she didn't care who knew. My eyes slid toward Mick, who had his own smile in celebration of catching the flirtatious exchange on film.

It was cold outside, but the sun had returned, and we trooped out to the barn for another morning of EVP sessions. Rob and Joseph headed to the old cabins to do some research there, and I was grateful for their absence. Carter and I would have to rope our own revenants, but it was a good excuse to take a quick look around the barn.

Beard, Nosy, Redneck, and Granny were the only ones there. The child was either still on the loose or being held somewhere else.

We started with Granny, leading her out to the fenced

enclosure without any problems. We turned on the tape recorder just in case, but my first words to her were, "You are dead. You died quite some time ago. You are a ghost."

"There is nothing to be afraid of. Your time here is done, and now you need to move on," Carter picked up. It still surprised me to hear how kind and gentle his voice was when he was trying to convince a spirit to cross over. If only he could be that nice all the time. "Your family wants you to be at peace, and so do we. Do you see the light? Move toward it. You already died, and there will be no pain and nothing to fear there on the other side."

Granny's body started to sway slowly, rhythmically. As Carter continued speaking, her swaying increased. Soon she was gyrating in wide circles, and Carter had to step backward to keep from being hit by her head each time she rotated forward.

Finally, Granny rocked violently toward Carter, her mouth opening to allow a sound like air escaping from a balloon to come out. She continued to fall forward, landing facedown on the ground.

Carter and I just stood there watching for a few minutes. Granny never moved. Carter let out a long breath, not unlike Granny's final exhale. "I've never seen anything like that before," he said.

"At least she's gone. Do we bury her now or wait for Rob and Joseph to come help?"

"Let's wait. It's not like waiting an hour will make her smell any worse."

It felt wrong to just leave the old woman's dead body on the ground like that. As a compromise, I pulled a blue tarp off the top of a log pile and threw it over Granny. At least we wouldn't have to look at her.

We continued our EVP sessions, questioning first Beard and then Redneck. We ended with Nosy, but we still couldn't ask him questions about being a demon hunter with Dwayne and Mick listening to our every word. Instead, I took a different tack. "How did you get to this island? How many of you are there here?" I asked.

Carter didn't realize what I was doing, and he said sardonically, "There are three left, Betty. Do you really need a zombie to do the math for you?"

"I'm just trying to ask questions that might generate a response," I said, tilting my head and raising my eyebrows at Carter.

"Oh." He blinked, then returned my look. "*Oh.*"

"Exactly."

Carter joined the line of questioning, asking, "Are we in danger here?" I wasn't sure why we would be, or why a revenant would have the answer, but after my adventure in the rain, it didn't seem like a stupid question at all.

My stomach was growling by the time we escorted Nosy back to the barn, and Rob and Joseph showed up as we replaced the lock on the door. "I'm starving," I announced.

"We have a body to bury," Carter reminded me.

"You had some success?" Joseph asked, eyeing the tarp I'd spread over Granny.

Carter and I filled Joseph and Rob in on Granny's odd departure. "Let's bury her after lunch," Joseph suggested. "No point in doing it right now when we're all hungry." Rob led the way back to the lodge, and Joseph fell into step beside me. "Well done, Betty," he said. Joseph reached for my hand, but I pulled away, keenly conscious of the cameras and of my newfound distrust for anyone on the island besides Carter.

"Carter is the king of crossing over spirits," I said. "He's really good at it."

"I'm sure you both deserve the congratulations. Perhaps we can take another walk this afternoon, and you can tell me all the details."

I glanced at Joseph and he caught my eye, his intent written boldly on his face. It wasn't just distrust that made me shy away from him, I realized. It was also Maxwell's visit from the night before. Yes, Joseph had stirred some feelings in me, but nothing like what I felt for Maxwell. Last night, I had felt so wonderfully protected, happy, and content in Maxwell's arms. Joseph, I knew, could only ever be a temporary reprieve for me. I still loved Maxwell, and now I knew that he still cared about me. I was mulling over my thoughts for so long that Joseph prompted me with an impatient, "Well?"

I blinked, realizing that I was still staring at Joseph even though his face wasn't the one I was seeing in my mind. "Maybe," I said. "We'll see how long it takes Carter and me to review all of this morning's EVP sessions."

We were halfway through the review of Redneck's EVP session when I began to hear strange sounds. As usual, Carter and I were sprawled on his bed. I was tired from burying Granny, and the cold shower I'd taken afterward had only made my muscles tighter. Cold was a word I no longer wanted in my vocabulary, and I was considering what tropical locations might be good for a ghost hunter when a distant moan snapped me out of my reverie.

"Carter, did your headphones come unplugged?" I asked.

"What?" he said, lifting one earpiece away from his head.

"I heard something, like a moan."

"It wasn't on here. Redneck hasn't said a word yet."

Maybe I was hearing things. I was making a mental pros and cons list for the Bahamas when I heard the moaning again. I sat up and pulled the headphones off Carter's head. "Listen," I hissed.

A moment later, I heard the moan a third time.

"The ghost?" Carter asked.

"Maybe. It sounds like it's in the hallway."

Carter thought to grab his tape recorder and camera before we went into the hallway. The moan was louder this time, and it sounded like it was coming from the other side of the staircase.

"Step carefully," Carter warned. "Remember, Stryker said that wing was dangerous from all the rotting boards."

I gave a mock salute but remained quiet so we could continue tracking the sound. The north wing was full of shadows, but there was enough light to see the rotten patches on the floor. Carter and I moved slowly and carefully, giving a wide berth to a steady drip coming from the ceiling. The water, probably from the storm the night before, had formed a big puddle on the floor in front of the second bedroom. The ceiling had clearly been leaking for a long time, and it had partially collapsed. I could see the rafters of the attic through a gaping hole in the plaster. It was only a matter of time before the steady leak disintegrated the floor, too.

As we got closer to the far end of the hallway, the moaning stopped. "We came to see you," Carter said. "If you're here, please give us a sign."

Nothing happened.

"Did you bring us all the way here just to leave? We want to help you," I said.

The moan sounded again, coming from somewhere on our right. "It's inside one of those bedrooms," Carter said, indicating two adjacent doors. "You take the left one, I'll take the right one. Don't go too far in; just listen for the moaning. Whichever room it's coming from is where we'll have an EVP session."

"Got it." I opened the left-hand door and crept inside. The floorboards creaked loudly, and I realized that I was probably the first person to tread on them in years. I stopped moving but didn't hear the moaning again. I took two more tentative steps inside the room and was struck with the musty, rotten smell of the place. The sun glowed through chinks in the old shutters, showing me a rusted iron bed and a mattress that had turned black with mold.

I heard another sound, but this wasn't a moan. It sounded more like crying, although it was soft and labored. "Who's there?" I asked. I walked forward a few steps. "Are you sad? Are you hurt?"

I didn't have a tape recorder with me, and I shouldn't be investigating alone anyway, I realized. I turned on my heel. "Carter," I called softly, "in here!" There was no response, so I took a step toward the door.

"Carter," I began again, just as there was a loud creak under my feet. I stepped backward out of surprise, but that was, apparently, the wrong direction. My feet came down on a rotten patch of wood, and they kept going right through the floor.

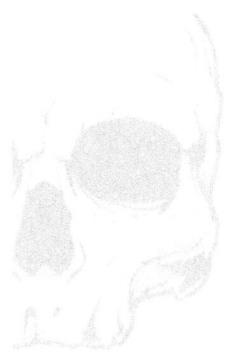

TWELVE

I screamed, my feet crashing through the plaster ceiling of the room below me. My fingers clutched at the floor as I desperately tried to stop my fall, and I felt a sudden, sharp pain in my side.

There was another stab of pain, this time in my back, and I abruptly stopped moving. I was stuck. The floorboards had broken apart only enough to let my torso fall through, and my shoulders were too wide to fit through the hole. My feet were still moving, looking for traction in the empty air, and I forced myself to stay still. The last thing I wanted was for the hole to gape further. It would be a long fall to the floor below, and there was no telling what I might land on.

"Oh, my God." It was Carter's voice, but when I glanced up and saw him in the doorway, I realized that he wasn't even looking at me. His attention was fixated on something behind me.

I tried to crane my neck around, but that only served to make the pain in my back sharper. "What, Carter?"

Carter's voice was low when he answered. "It's the child," he said.

"That's impossible. There was no one here when I looked in."

"I think he was hiding in the bathroom."

"Carter, get me out of this hole, and then we can deal with the revenant."

Carter finally turned his attention to me. "Oh, yeah, of course. Geez, Betty, how did you do this to yourself?"

"Just help me."

Carter took my hands and tried hauling me up, but it was too awkward to be effective. He dropped to his knees instead and wrapped his arms under mine. "On the count of three," he said. "One, two, three!" On three, Carter yanked up and backwards, and I felt myself rise. Now I was only stuck from the waist down, but after one more pull my legs cleared the floor. I scrambled away from the rotten patch and sank down onto my knees. My legs were shaking too badly for me to stand.

"You're hurt," Carter said.

"No, I'm just feeling a little unsteady. I'll be fine once I realize that I'm not actually going to fall to my death today."

"No, you're hurt." Carter reached toward me and lifted the hem of my—well, his—sweater. I looked down and saw the blood seeping from a cut on my side. "We'll have to look at this in the light. I bet you've got a dozen splinters in that cut."

I groaned. Falling to my death might have been a better choice.

A soft moan reminded us that we weren't alone. I looked up and saw the child standing in front of the bed. His languid eyes were unfocused, their color a dull blue. The boy's hair stuck out in wild tangles, and his clothes hung loosely, like he had been a lot fuller when he was alive. There was something strangely familiar about him, but I couldn't place what.

"How did he get up here?" I asked.

"How did you get down there?" Carter retorted,

pointing at the hole in the floor. "You know you have to be careful in this wing."

"Spare me the lecture, Carter. I assure you, I wasn't tap-dancing across the floor." I shifted and had to grit my teeth at the stab of pain in my back. "I think I have another cut over my right shoulder blade."

Carter leaned over me. "You've got a chunk of floor sticking out of your back. Hang on; this is going to hurt." Without further warning, Carter yanked the wood out of my skin. I shrieked at the flare of pain. "I'm going to be picking splinters out of you for an hour. And my new sweater is ruined. Do you have any idea how much that cost?"

I bit my lip, though I'm sure Carter could see how annoyed I was with him. He wisely changed the subject. "What are we going to do about the pint-sized zombie?"

"I guess we should try to talk to him."

Carter pulled out his tape recorder and got no further than, "What is your name?" when we heard Joseph's voice behind us. He came running into the room and stopped short when he saw Carter and me sitting on the floor. "What happened?" he asked. "Betty, you screamed."

"I tried to go high-diving, but Carter stopped me," I said, pointing at the floor.

Joseph gaped, then dropped to his knees and took my hands in mine. "Are you hurt?"

I tried to shrug, but it hurt, and I winced. "I got a little torn up by the splintered boards, but I'll live."

"Besides, we have bigger problems than Betty ruining my sweater," Carter chimed in. Joseph looked up at him, then followed Carter's gesture toward the boy.

"It's a kid." Joseph's voice was flat. "One of *them*."

"Yes, and somehow he wandered in here," I said. "We heard his moans and thought it was the ghost."

Joseph turned his attention back to me. "Did he push you into the hole?"

"No, that was my own doing. I didn't even realize someone else was in the room with me."

Joseph frowned, his gaze shifting from me, to Carter, to the revenant. Eventually he said, "I'll go get the rope so we can take it out to the barn."

"Aren't you at all concerned with where he came from?" I asked. "How is it that another revenant has been wandering the island this whole time, and no one knew?"

"Well, I see that Carter has his tape recorder out. Perhaps you can ask the child." Joseph gave my hands a gentle squeeze. "I'll be back shortly."

Joseph was gone for twenty minutes, and we used the time to conduct an EVP session with the boy. The revenant never moved while we spoke to him, and he didn't make a sound.

"What are we going to name this one?" Carter asked as he turned off his tape recorder.

"Near Death Experience."

"Very funny."

"Junior?"

"That works." Carter started to say something else, but he stopped at the sound of footsteps in the hall. Joseph entered a moment later, followed closely by Rob. They were both carrying the poles and ropes used to lead the revenants.

Rob's eyes were wide behind his glasses. "So unsafe here, so unsafe," he said. He said it more to himself than to us.

"Don't worry, Rob, Betty already found the weak spots. She can tell you where not to walk." Carter's smile was teasing.

My back and side hurt, but my foot didn't, and I gladly

jabbed Carter with my toe. "Any idea where Junior came from?" I asked Rob.

Rob nervously rubbed his hand over the back of his neck. "They just keep showing up, don't they? How many more are out there that we don't know about yet?"

How did Rob and Joseph manage to work together? They were such opposites in everything: appearance, personality, and, clearly, bravery.

I assured Rob that we'd find out what else was lurking on the island, though my words were interrupted with groans as I stood to move out of their way. Joseph appraised me thoroughly. "I'll help get you patched up once we get this thing to the barn."

I waved him off. "No, it's not as bad as that. I'll be fine."

The child put up no resistance when Rob and Joseph looped the ropes over his head. They led him carefully around the hole in the floor and slowly brought him into the hallway.

"You sure you'll be okay?" Joseph asked one last time.

"I'm sure."

Joseph gave a curt nod before he and Rob tackled the challenge of getting Junior down the stairs. As they descended, Carter followed me back to my room. I fished my tweezers out of my make-up bag, but Carter decided it was too dark in my room to really see well. Instead, he led me onto the balcony. I hiked my sweater up and leaned over the railing so Carter could start picking the splinters out of the cut on my side.

It hurt, a lot, and there was nothing I could do but put up with the pain. I kept my jaw clenched while Carter worked, but I still let out a few grunts and groans during the process.

When Carter declared that cut splinter-free, he instructed me to take off my sweater so he could work on the cut on my shoulder blade. "Out here in broad daylight?" I asked.

"Betty, it's not like there are a lot of people who are going to see."

I had no choice but to acquiesce. I pulled the sweater off and stood there on the balcony in my bra. I was embarrassed, cold, and in pain. I was definitely having a lousy day.

The chunk of wood that had lodged in my skin had left a bevy of splinters, and it took Carter a lot longer to get all of them out. By the time he was done, my arms were covered in goose bumps and my fingertips were feeling numb. "All right," Carter instructed. "Go lay on your bed, and I'll find some alcohol and bandages."

Carter let himself out of my room while I eased down onto my stomach. He was gone long enough that I actually began to doze off. Carter swabbed alcohol onto my cuts, which woke me up thoroughly. It stung nearly as much as getting the injuries themselves had.

After what seemed like an eternity, I was bandaged. "Where are your shirts?" Carter asked.

"Piled on top of my suitcase," I said, pointing. Carter nudged me a moment later, and I sat up to put on the proffered shirt. "I'm sorry about your sweater," I mumbled.

"It's okay. There are more where it came from." Carter sat distractedly.

My voice was even quieter when I spoke again. "And thank you for rescuing me."

Carter just observed me silently. I put my hand over his. "Thank you," I said again, my tone firmer.

In answer, Carter just said, "I don't think Junior showed up by chance."

"Mick and Dwayne weren't even there to film it, so I guess that rules out them trying to surprise us."

"But why would Rob or Stryker plant the kid there? It

makes no sense." Carter stood and sighed. "I'm going to go listen to the rest of today's EVP sessions. I'll let you know if I find anything. Get some rest."

Carter paused before he closed my door behind him. "Oh, and Betty? You're welcome."

I curled up under my blanket, but not until I'd gotten up and locked my door behind Carter. I didn't want any other roaming revenants to catch me unaware. My brain wouldn't settle down, so instead of sleeping, I wound up going through possible scenarios over and over again. I could come up with no logical reason why Junior had showed up in the lodge, other than it just being a coincidence. Maybe whoever had followed him the night before hadn't been able to catch him, and Junior had finally wandered over to our side of the island. And then, somehow, he'd opened the front door of the lodge and climbed the stairs, all without anyone noticing.

It didn't seem all that likely, but it was the best I had.

Carter knocked on my door some time later, and he looked pleased with himself as I ushered him inside. "Grant Tucker," he said smugly.

"Who?"

"Grant Tucker. It's the name that Redneck gave us when you asked who had shot him."

"Oh, good. Now that we know, maybe we can get some results with him."

Carter nodded. "I think we should go out there now. We should have enough time before dinner."

"We may as well. I can't sleep, and getting a little sunshine might do me some good. But I'm going to have to borrow more clothes from you."

Carter grimaced, but before heading to the barn, we

stopped in his room. "Try not to ruin this one," he said, handing me a red hoodie emblazoned with the East Coast Paranormal Authorities logo. I made a face of mock disgust as I put it on.

We were halfway down the porch steps when Dwayne hailed us. "Where are you two going?"

"To the barn," Carter said. "Grab your camera and come on."

While Dwayne retrieved his gear, Carter and I had to run into the kitchen for our mics. We had put them back on the chargers after lunch. Adrienne was there, already working on dinner, and she greeted Carter warmly. "I'm working on a special dessert just for you," she said, winking.

"Was I ever that bad with Maxwell?" I asked as we finally started toward the barn.

"You did tend to get a little moon-eyed whenever he was around."

"Betty, can you tell us who Maxwell is?" Dwayne asked.

I'd completely forgotten about the microphone already. I turned and looked right into Dwayne's camera. "Just an ex-boyfriend."

When we reached the barn, Beard was sprawled backwards over a pile of old lumber inside the door. His legs were twisted at an odd angle, like he'd tripped and fallen. I held my handkerchief tight against my nose and mouth as I approached: Beard smelled worse than ever.

"I think he's dead," I said, my words muffled.

Carter came up beside me and lowered his own handkerchief briefly. "I think he's dead."

"That's what I said!"

I had no idea why Beard's ghost had decided to cross over. Maybe he had finally realized he was dead (the burst belly was a dead giveaway, after all), or maybe he had simply given up on trying to get a message across to us. Either way, I was glad to know he had moved on and would finally be at peace. I was also glad to know that I wouldn't have to look at his entrails any longer. I actually felt eager about burying Beard, just to have him out of my sight forever.

With Beard gone, that left just Redneck, Nosy, and Junior. The latter, I noticed, was hunkered down in one corner, the same sad combination of crying and moaning escaping his lips every now and then.

Even with the number of residents in the barn dwindling, I still felt a lot more comfortable once we were outside, with only Redneck to contend with. "We know that Grant Tucker shot you," Carter said. "We know he murdered you."

Redneck blinked, and his eyes snapped into focus. He started at Carter, who repeated, "We know it was Grant Tucker who shot you."

Something like relief came over Redneck's slack face, and it looked like the corners of his mouth turned up ever so slightly before he crumpled to the ground.

"That was easy," I said.

"Not really. It did take a few tries to figure out what his ghost was hanging around for."

"Yeah, but he wasn't nearly as stubborn as Nosy."

Neither Nosy nor Junior had given us any answers to our questions, so our work was done for the day. On the upside, two ghosts had crossed over today. On the downside, we had another revenant on our hands. I had also fallen through the floor, and my cold-weather clothes were still soaking wet. I was chilly even in Carter's sweatshirt, but it was better than nothing.

Carter and I gladly shared our news about Beard and Redneck over dinner, and Joseph and Rob seemed suitably impressed. Rob, I noticed, was a little jumpy, and he kept checking over his shoulder like he'd find a revenant standing there. He was certainly a timid, paranoid type.

We lingered long after Adrienne had cleared our dinner plates, discussing Junior's sudden appearance and the possibility that there were other revenants we hadn't discovered yet. Carter, I noticed, had still not gotten his special dessert. Maybe Adrienne was waiting to serve it to him when the rest of us were gone.

Carter and Rob both made a beeline for the stairs when we decided to call it a night. Joseph, though, stopped me in the lobby. "Are you feeling all right after your fall?" he asked.

"I'm all right. Carter got all the splinters out of me, and the actual cuts weren't that bad."

"I didn't just mean the injuries. You had quite a scare today, both from the fall and from finding, ah, Junior, I believe you called him."

I paused, thinking. Strangely, I did feel all right. The fall had been much more frightening than Junior's appearance—especially since I'd already encountered him once before—and now I knew to be extra-cautious if I went into any unused areas of the lodge. "I'm good," I assured Joseph.

Joseph reached for my hand, but this time he didn't let me pull away. His fingers entwined tightly with mine. "Do you want me to stay with you tonight?"

"I'll be fine."

Joseph brought my hand to his lips and kissed each finger, slowly. "Then maybe you'd like to come to my room for a while." When I began to protest, he raised his free hand to silence me. "Don't worry, I won't try anything you're not comfortable with. I just thought we could grab a bottle of wine from the kitchen, curl up in bed, and keep each other warm for a while."

Adrienne chose that moment to walk past us, heading

up the stairs while balancing a slice of cherry pie, two glasses, and a bottle of champagne. I blushed, knowing she had seen the way Joseph and I were standing and the way his lips were still fluttering against my fingers.

"I really shouldn't," I said, slowly untangling my hand. "I think I had enough wine at dinner."

Joseph's eyebrows knit together. "Suit yourself, Betty. I thought you'd feel safer with me." Joseph spun around and marched upstairs without another word. I thought about calling after him, but I didn't know what to say. I wasn't comfortable with what he was proposing, but I certainly hadn't meant to anger him. No wonder I loved Maxwell. He wasn't nearly as difficult to date as a human was.

I was alone in the lobby, and only one oil lamp was still burning. I picked it up so I wouldn't have to climb the stairs in the dark, but I changed direction before I reached the staircase. I turned right and walked into the room behind the check-in desk.

I found myself in some kind of ballroom. Like the lobby, the room had intricate chandeliers hanging overhead, and matching sconces lined the walls. The wallpaper had probably been beautiful before its flocked velvet had become faded and water-stained. A few tables were grouped in one corner, and there was a stage at the far end. It looked spooky in the dim light of my oil lamp, but I pressed on. I was curious to see where I would have landed if I'd fallen completely through the floor.

The hole I'd made in the ceiling was easy enough to find, even in the dark. Below, bits of wood and plaster were scattered across a buffet table. Well, I consoled myself, the table would have broken my fall. And then I glanced under the table and saw the boxes stacked there. The cardboard was old and dirty, but the labels on each were clear. One said "champagne flutes" and the other, "brandy snifters." I peeked inside one of the boxes, and it was full of glassware. I felt a wave of gratitude toward Carter for pulling me to safety. Picking splinters out of my skin was one thing, pulling out shards of glass was another.

I sighed, feeling the release of anxiety that I hadn't even realized I felt. Now that I knew what might have happened, I decided that my day hadn't been so awful after all.

My foot was on the first stair when a voice spoke behind me. "He always does this, you know." I turned and saw Rob standing just a few feet from me, his face shiny in the glow of my lamp.

"Who does what?"

"Joseph. He's the ladies man, always flirting. At least one girl falls for it everywhere we go."

"Oh, I don't know, I think I've been pretty good at not letting him get to me." I tried to make my tone light, but Rob's sudden appearance had startled me. I continued walking, but he followed me up the stairs.

"It's just that you need to watch out for yourself," Rob continued. "You might get hurt."

"Don't worry. I'm not giving away my heart that easily."

"I didn't mean that kind of hurt."

Before I could turn around, Rob grabbed my wrists and bent my arms behind my back. The oil lamp fell to the floor, shattering as the flame snuffed out. Rob had more strength than I would have guessed, and no matter how much I squirmed, I couldn't get out of his grip. His breath was hot on my neck as he pushed me up the stairs in front of him. I stumbled again and again in the sudden dark, and each time Rob's grip grew tighter.

Rob deftly held my wrists with one hand, and when something pricked my side, I knew he'd drawn a knife. I was so shocked that I couldn't even react initially, but I began to fight back in earnest when we reached the second floor. I stuck my leg behind me, hoping I could catch Rob's foot and trip him, but the knife only pushed harder against my skin, and I knew it was close to drawing blood.

I stopped straining against him immediately, unsure what to do. Rob assumed that I'd given up completely, and he walked me toward the door to his bedroom. "That's a good girl," he whispered. His breathing was heavy, and I could smell the wine on his breath. "Now open the door for me."

I reached forward, then paused. My chances of escaping would diminish if he got me inside his room. I took a deep breath, steeled myself against the pain the knife would bring, and screamed, "Carter, help! Help! Joseph!"

Carter and Joseph had both come upstairs, and I knew they were just feet away, in their own rooms.

But no one came to my rescue.

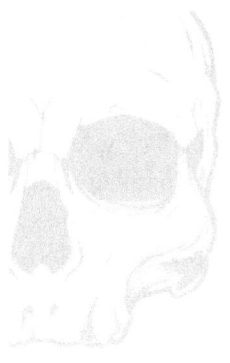

THIRTEEN

Rob gave the knife a shove when I shouted, and I felt its sting against my skin, followed by a trickle of blood down my side. Even amidst the fear, I had a brief wave of guilt for ruining another piece of Carter's wardrobe.

"Scream again, and the knife goes in all the way," Rob said. "Now open the door."

My hand trembled as I grasped the doorknob, and I turned it as slowly as I could to delay the inevitable. As soon as the door opened a crack, Rob propelled me over the threshold and slammed the door behind him.

I didn't know what to do. Now that I was trapped in the room, I felt the fear begin to control me. My chest heaved as I tried to draw air, and sweat broke out on my face.

Rob stopped abruptly at the foot of his bed. In one movement, he spun me around, pushed me onto the bed, and brought the knife down against my other side. He leaned over me, and he was sweating so profusely that his glasses were slowly sliding down his nose. Rob was nervous, just as he had been at dinner. He kept glancing away, then back at me. Still, I could tell that I wasn't the first person he'd held at knifepoint. He might be anxious, but the hand holding the knife was steady.

"No more screaming, got it?" he said. I felt his oversized stomach pressing against me as he lay down on top of me. I turned my face away as he leaned in, and his lips brushed my ear as he said, "You just stay still, and everything will be okay."

I stifled a scream just as Rob looked away, his body tense. There were no lights on in the room and no fire, and it was too dark to see anything more than a foot or two away from me. Rob was searching so hard for something in the darkness that he shifted, and I felt the knife sink into my side. This time, I couldn't keep my scream from escaping.

"Shut up!" Rob yelled. He twisted the knife sharply as he spoke. The pain was awful, but I was too afraid to cry out again.

Rob's nervousness was increasing; I could practically feel it radiating from his body. He leaned up and shouted, "Come on. Come on!"

I didn't know who or what he was talking to, but something decided to accept his invitation. Rob's body was yanked off mine, and I heard a loud crack. Rob groaned loudly, then fell silent.

In fact, the entire room was eerily silent. I couldn't hear anything but my own breathing. I lay quietly for a moment, still too afraid to move. Rob, I suspected, was no longer a threat, but something had heaved him across the room. That same something might attack me next. Had it been Joseph or Carter? No. If it had been, they would have come forward to help me by now.

I considered that it might be the ghost Adrienne had seen in her room. Perhaps he'd stepped in to defend me. I sat up and listened hard, but the room was still silent. It was too quiet for someone else to be in the room with me, and I decided that the ghost must have come to my rescue.

When I rose to my feet, my knees were so shaky that I had to sit down on the edge of the bed. My left foot bumped against something, and I reached down to find out what. It was Rob's foot. Slowly, I shifted into a crouching position on the floor and followed the outline of his prone body. My fingers felt their way up to his shoulders. Above that, there was something warm and wet on the floor. Blood, I suspected. The crack I had heard had probably been Rob's head hitting the mantle above the fireplace.

Tentatively, I put a hand over Rob's chest and felt the shallow rise and fall of his breathing. Still alive. I was mildly disappointed at that. At least he was unconscious.

I moved slowly to the door of his room, still too shaky to walk without supporting myself against the wall. The hallway was dark, but I knew my way to Carter's room. I pounded on the door, calling his name, but there was no answer. I tried Joseph's room next, with the same response. I even knocked on Adrienne's door, thinking that maybe Carter was sleeping in there. No one answered, and I felt utterly alone.

I slunk into my room, locking the door behind me. There was a box of matches on my nightstand, and soon I had two oil lamps burning. I didn't expect Rob to renew his efforts when he awoke, but just in case, I slid the antique trunk in front of the balcony door. Every time I pushed on the trunk, I felt the sharp pain in my side where Rob's knife had penetrated. I was afraid to look down to see how badly I was bleeding.

I pushed my nightstand against the door to the hallway, though I knew it would do little good if someone really wanted to get in my room. To give myself even more of a barrier, I carried both oil lamps into the bathroom and locked the door behind me. With nothing left to do, I finally turned my attention to my newest wounds.

The cut on my right side, from when I'd shouted for help, wasn't any worse than the cuts I'd gotten during my fall through the floor earlier. This time, at least, there were no splinters to contend with. Thankfully, Carter had left extra bandages with me, and that cut was quickly patched.

The second wound was much deeper, and my blood had soaked Carter's sweatshirt before trickling down to stain the top of my jeans, too. If I weren't on a deserted island, I probably would have gone to the emergency room for stitches. Instead, I folded a washcloth and pressed it tight against my side to slow the bleeding.

I sat down on the cold tile floor, my back against the bathtub so that I could face the door. No noise reached my ears, though every second I expected to hear Rob trying to beat down my door. I was still in too much shock to cry or scream, or any of the other reactions that seemed like a normal response to what I'd just endured.

I fell asleep at some point, still sitting upright but too exhausted to stay conscious any longer.

Loud knocking on the door brought me out of my doze, and after a brief moment of confusion, the night's events came flooding back to me. I jumped to my feet, realizing that by hiding in the bathroom, I'd backed myself into a corner and had no means of escape.

When the knocking came again, I realized that it was on the door to my room, not the bathroom. I opened the bathroom door tentatively and heard my name being called. It was Carter, and he sounded like he was half asleep.

I moved my nightstand out of the way and opened my door. As soon as Carter was inside, I shut it, locked it, and put the nightstand in place once again.

"What's going on?" Carter mumbled. His eyes were lidded, and he yawned widely. "I dreamed that you were knocking on my door and calling for help. When I woke up, it all felt too real. I wanted to check on you, just in case."

"It was Rob," I said, my voice barely above a whisper.

"He pulled a knife and made me go into his room. I think he was going to—" I stopped, unable to say the word "rape." The reality of what might have happened hit me suddenly and completely, and I covered my face as I began to cry.

Carter's arms instantly pulled me to him in a hug, but his voice was fierce, all traces of drowsiness gone. "Did he hurt you?"

"He stabbed me," I said, stuttering amid my heaving breaths. I pulled away and lifted the side of my sweatshirt. "I'm sorry; I'll replace it, I promise."

"Don't be silly."

I inhaled sharply when Carter put his fingers against the wound, but was relieved when he said that the blood had dried. "Where is that bastard now?"

"Hopefully still unconscious on the floor." I told him about Rob's nervous behavior and how something had pulled him off me. "I think it was the ghost," I concluded. "There was no one else in the room with us."

"It's entirely possible."

"Carter, what am I supposed to do?"

Carter bit his lip, thinking. His tone was disappointed but determined when he finally spoke. "We have to leave. You can't stay here with someone who's trying to assault you. We'll tell Joseph first thing in the morning, and he can take us back to the mainland in the boat."

"What about Nosy and Junior? They still need our help."

"Your safety is more important than a couple of ghosts." Carter put his hands on my shoulders and gave me an exasperated look. "For God's sake, Betty, you were stabbed tonight, and if it weren't for that ghost, a knife wound would have been the least of your worries."

I shut my eyes. "You're right. I'm just not thinking

straight. It's been a really long day, and I'm tired of getting holes poked in my body."

Carter gave me a nudge toward my bed, and I obediently scooted under the covers. I took off my shoes first but didn't bother changing out of my bloody clothes. Carter retrieved the oil lamps from the bathroom, and he left one of them burning on my nightstand. I expected him to go back to his own room, but instead he sat down next to me, his back against the headboard.

"You sticking around?" I asked.

"There's no way I'm leaving you alone after what happened."

That made me feel much better, and I could already feel sleep tugging at my weary mind. Before I gave in to it, though, I had one more thing to ask Carter. "How could you not have heard me earlier? I was screaming for help, and neither you nor Joseph heard me."

"I don't know. Adrienne came up to my room, and I wound up falling asleep. I don't even remember her leaving. I guess I was just really tired."

"It's just weird that neither of you came to help."

"Good thing the ghost came to your rescue."

"Yeah." I closed my eyes, and the next time I opened them, sunlight was streaming through the window. I rolled over as every muscle protested and saw Carter still sitting next to me. His head was tilted back against the headboard, and I heard his gentle snoring.

I quietly got up and went into the bathroom for a shower. My side had bled some more during the night, but at least the rest of my cuts looked like they were scabbing over.

My wardrobe was quickly diminishing. I put on a fresh pair of jeans and a long-sleeved tee. Hopefully this outfit would survive the day without any bloodstains.

Adrienne knocked on the door and called good

morning soon after my shower, and Carter cracked one eye open. "Ready to go home?" he mumbled.

"I can be packed in three seconds," I promised.

Carter rose and stretched. "I'll go talk to Joseph. You stay here. There's no point in you risking a run-in with Rob."

I wasn't going to argue that.

Even from the confines of my room, I knew that Carter's news did not go over well with Joseph. I heard a shout, followed by the sound of angry footsteps and heavy pounding. Joseph was, I surmised, knocking on Rob's door to confront him. I wondered if Rob was still sprawled on the floor.

I didn't have to wonder for long. There was more shouting, this time of surprise, and then a knock on my door.

Carter and Joseph looked almost comical in their shock. "He's dead," Carter said.

"What? He was alive when I left him last night. He was unconscious, but he was breathing." I looked from one face to the other, hoping I'd find some answers there.

"I think you need to see this for yourself." Carter took my arm and led me to Rob's room. Joseph followed silently.

I averted my eyes when we went into Rob's room. I wasn't exactly looking forward to seeing another dead body, but Carter said, "Look."

I glanced toward the fireplace briefly, knowing I'd see Rob's body there.

Except I didn't. My head snapped up again. The blood from Rob's head wound was still there, but his body wasn't. I looked all around the room, but there was no sign of him, alive or dead.

"There's nothing there," I said.

"Look again."

I stepped forward, feeling as if someone was playing a joke on me. There was no dead body in the room, so what was I supposed to be looking for?

And then I saw it. Just a few traces of blackened ashes, scattered on the floor in front of the fireplace.

"It's probably from the fireplace," I said quietly, but I knew it wasn't.

Joseph broke his silence at last. "Rob was killed by a demon," he said.

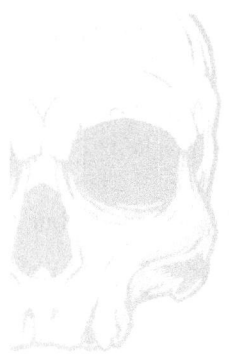

FOURTEEN

Two thoughts struck me at once. First, I knew without a doubt that Maxwell had been the demon responsible for killing Rob. That also meant that his nighttime visit to my room had been real and not just the product of a nearly-frozen imagination.

The other, very sobering thought I had was that Joseph recognized a demon attack. Few people knew that demons could incinerate a body, leaving just ashes. A man in Joseph's line of work should have no reason to know such things.

Before I could articulate either of these thoughts, I heard a click. When I turned, I saw that Joseph had a gun in his hand. "Stryker," Carter said, "what are you doing?"

"My partner is dead," Joseph said. "I'm a little angry right now."

"Don't you understand what he tried to do to Betty last night? You're lucky she didn't kill him herself." Carter's tone was incredulous.

Joseph didn't answer. Instead, he pounded his fist against the wall and shouted, "Adrienne!"

The woman appeared quickly, looking unsurprised to see Joseph holding us at gunpoint. "Yes?" she asked calmly.

"Get those men and their cameras off the island right now. Make up an excuse."

Adrienne smiled vaguely at us. As she turned and walked away, her voice trailed back to us. "Oh, Carter, I am so glad you enjoyed your dessert last night."

Carter's hands balled into fists. "She drugged me. That little bitch."

"But why would she do that?" I gasped as the answer popped into my head. "So you couldn't rescue me. She knew that Rob was going to attack me last night."

"You're very clever, Betty," Joseph said.

"At least Carter has an excuse for not helping me last night. What's yours?"

Joseph laughed disdainfully. "I'm the one who told Rob to do it. I was hoping that putting you in danger would bring your dear ex-boyfriend out of hiding." Joseph shook his head slowly. "Unfortunately, the plan was a little too successful."

"I don't understand. You were trying to get Maxwell to attack Rob?"

"Yes. And Rob was supposed to stab him with that knife and send him back to hell. When I heard you screaming last night, I knew there was no reason to come to your rescue. Your cries simply meant that everything was going according to plan."

I had once found Joseph so attractive, but looking at him now, all I felt was disgust. To think that he was willing to compromise me like that just to catch a demon made my skin crawl. Demon hunters—I was certain that's what Joseph was—were supposed to have some sort of moral code. They professed to be men of God, but clearly Joseph was willing to compromise ethics in the hope of banishing a demon.

Things still weren't making a whole lot of sense to me. "I knocked on your door after I got away from Rob. Shouldn't you have realized then that things had gone wrong? I mean, I got away."

Joseph sounded offended when he said, "Betty, have more faith in me. I never intended for Rob to go through with it. He was always supposed to let you get away once the demon showed up. I knew you'd be too scared to stay and welcome your lover back."

I shut my eyes. I had a lot of unanswered questions, but at the moment I was overwhelmed by guilt. Even after our breakup, I was still being used as a pathway to Maxwell. And Maxwell was still coming to my rescue. How had he known I was in danger? And how had he even known where I was?

"Here's what we're going to do," Joseph said, interrupting my thoughts. "As soon as Adrienne gets the others off the island, we're going to take a little walk to the barn. You two can sit in there and discuss the meaning of life with the zombies while we wait for the demon to make his heroic return."

"And then what? You're going to banish him?" I asked. "Rob wasn't good enough to do it. What makes you think you are?"

"Because I'm better than Rob. Always was. Still, he thought he could do it, so I let him have the chance. He failed."

Good riddance, I thought.

We stood in silence for a few moments. There were so many thoughts whirling through my head that I didn't even know where to start. Carter looked angry, and Joseph stood placidly, a smug smile on his face. Soon, we heard three quick beeps of a horn.

"Adrienne is away. That leaves just us, the zombies, and your darling demon," Joseph said. He backed out of the room, keeping the gun trained on us. "Right this way, if you please."

Carter and I had no choice but to obey. We were marched down the stairs, out of the lodge, and onto the trail that led to the barn. Halfway there, Carter said, "So you don't actually work for the National Trust?"

"Oh, I do. All three of us do. Demon hunting, sadly, is not a steady source of income. It's rare for a demon to fetch as much of a bounty as this Maxwell. This particular job gave us the perfect opportunity for luring him here. We knew that if Betty came and found herself in a compromising situation, then we'd have a good chance of catching him."

"How did you know Carter would bring me along?" I asked.

"I asked him to bring a companion and strongly suggested you," Joseph said. He sounded proud of himself for manipulating Carter. "I said that I'd seen you in pictures from investigations and that you seemed both competent and attractive enough for the reality show. I flattered Carter for teaming up with you in the past. We played to his ego, and it worked."

I glanced at Carter just in time to see him look away, his expression a mixture of anger and embarrassment. I quickly changed the subject, asking, "Adrienne is a hunter, too?" I just couldn't picture the nice woman, who had been so shaken up over the ghost in her room, confronting a demon.

"Her father was," Joseph said. "She didn't care to follow in his footsteps, but she wanted to support those who did. Her father was killed while trying to banish a demon."

I had no response to that. I was sorry that her father had died, and I knew that, for the most part, what demon hunters did was good: they rid the earth of evil creatures. Still, I took it personally when anyone went after Maxwell, and it was impossible to condone hunting that involved hurting innocent people, like me.

When we reached the barn door, Joseph instructed Carter to remove the lock. We went inside, and I had to pull my shirt up over my nose and mouth to combat the stench. Stay calm, I told myself.

I expected Joseph to shut the door and lock it, leaving us alone with the revenants. I was almost right. Before doing so, Joseph looked into my eyes. His voice was a little sad as he said, "I really did like you, Betty. It's too bad you chose to carouse with a servant of Satan. Otherwise, you're a really great girl, and I'm sorry I have to do this."

Joseph's gun was deafening in the confines of the barn, and I clamped my hands over my ears before I realized that my leg was suddenly in a great deal of pain. I looked down and saw the blood blossoming across the right leg of my jeans. A wave of dizziness washed over me, and I swayed. I felt Carter's arms catch me as Joseph's face disappeared behind the closing door.

Carter eased me onto the dirt floor, and I shouted a lot of expletives as I clamped a hand over the hole in my jeans. "He shot me," I said, again and again, as Carter shoved my hand away to inspect the wound for himself.

"He's doing everything he can to make sure Maxwell shows up," Carter said. "Stop touching it; I'm trying to see how bad it is. It's so damn dark in here."

I gasped and groaned as Carter prodded my leg. "It's a long gash. He got the side of your thigh, so the bullet didn't actually go in."

"Well, it still hurts like hell," I said through clenched teeth.

Carter was wearing pajama pants still, and I noticed for the first time that he was barefoot. He had, however, thrown on a sweatshirt before coming to my room the night before. Now, he took it off, folded it against my leg, and tied the arms around my thigh as a makeshift bandage.

"I fully expect to be shot again," I said.

"Why?"

I began counting off my injuries on my fingers. "Two cuts from falling through the floor and two cuts from Rob's knife. If injuries come in twos, then I'm in big trouble."

"Maybe getting shot counts double?"

Carter helped maneuver me into a sitting position against the wall of the barn. We could hear Joseph pacing back and forth outside the door, so there was no point in trying to get out.

"They brought the revenants here so they'd have an excuse to invite us," I conjectured.

"It looks like it," Carter said, settling down next to me. "And I'm guessing they planted Junior in the lodge on purpose. I'm sure they wanted Maxwell to come to your rescue instead of me."

"So Adrienne made sure you couldn't come to my rescue last night."

"And now we both need Maxwell to come rescue us," Carter concluded. As we sat, Nosy and Junior began to walk toward us slowly. "You knew something was odd when you realized that Nosy had been a hunter."

"They were using one of their own to lure us. That's awful. It's almost as bad as using the ghost of a child. I wonder where they got all the revenants from?"

I felt Carter's shoulder shrug against mine. "I don't know. I also wonder what this means for the pilot episode of the show."

"Really, Carter? We're locked in a barn with two revenants, I've been shot, and the maniac outside is planning to banish the demon that we hope comes to rescue us. With all of that, you still have room in that brain to worry about your TV show?"

"Yes."

I gave a short laugh.

"What's so funny?"

"You, Carter. No matter what kind of danger we're in,

or how absurd the situation gets, I can always count on you to be you. That's kind of comforting."

"I'd rather sit here and worry about the future of the TV show than sit here and worry about the future of my own life. I'm happily pretending that we're both going to get out of this in one piece."

"At least you're keeping a positive outlook."

As the morning dragged on, Carter and I came up with several escape plans, all of which we quickly rejected for one reason or another. Our plans ranged from the ridiculously simple—break down the door and wrestle Joseph's gun away from him—to the absolutely impossible—the craziest of which involved us both realizing we were comic book superheroes with great powers.

I was hungry, tired, dirty, and I'd lost a fair amount of blood over the past twenty-four hours. I was also cold and desperately missing my jacket. The smell emanating from the revenants was so putrid that neither Carter nor myself ever got used to it as the day wore on.

"I took vacation time for this, you know," I told Carter after my stomach gave a particularly loud grumble. "I also thought this would be a good way to get over Maxwell. Daisy was actually afraid I'd hook up with you on this trip."

Carter snorted derisively. "Not likely. You were far from being over Maxwell, and two weeks on an island certainly wasn't going to cure that."

"I had hoped it would."

"What you really need is—" Carter stopped and sat up straight. He put his hand against my arm, and I recognized the gesture as a way of telling me to be silent. Usually, that would mean Carter had heard something odd during a paranormal investigation. In this case, though, he'd picked up the sound of a voice outside.

All we could hear was the distant voice of a man. The

words were indecipherable, but the tone was angry. The speaker was coming closer to the barn, walking down the trail from the lodge to the clearing, I guessed. Soon, we could also hear a female voice, speaking excitedly. As the voices grew louder, I could make out some of the words.

"...saying is that...no right," I heard the woman say.

"What? That was...hurt," the man responded.

Now I heard Joseph's voice clearly. "What are you doing here?"

"He was at the boat dock on the mainland. I told him not to come back with me, but he insisted." I recognized Adrienne's voice. She sounded apologetic and indignant all at once.

"I got a phone call that Betty was in danger." The man's voice was clear now, and I recognized it at once. I turned around and looked for a gap in the boards so I could see out. All I saw were weeds growing in front of the barn, but it didn't matter. I knew Lou's voice when I heard it.

"Someone called you?" Joseph said suspiciously. "We don't even have a cell signal out here. I think you just came because you were worried you wouldn't get your share of the money." Joseph's voice rose. "You've got a thing or two to learn about being a hunter. When someone like me gives you their word, you trust it. Showing up like this is a quick way to make sure no other hunter wants to work with you in the future."

Lou didn't back down. "I got a phone call that Betty was being hurt. That was never a part of our deal. I specifically said that she was not to be in any kind of danger."

I leaned my head against the wall and shut my eyes. Lou was working with Joseph, Adrienne, and Rob. The man who had once been one of my closest friends was now using me to hunt down Maxwell. "Oh, Lou, no," I whispered.

When I turned my attention to the conversation once again, Joseph was telling Lou that I was fine. I didn't know that getting shot put one in the "doing fine" category. "The revenants are harmless. Betty only got hurt because she fell through a rotten patch of wood on the second floor of the lodge. It could have happened to any of us," Joseph lied.

"Then let me see her," Lou said.

"The last I checked, you didn't want her to know that you were working with us."

"I just need to know that she's okay."

There was a loud bang on the door of the barn. "Betty, tell your *friend* out here that you're all right," Joseph said loudly.

"Lou! You have to get me out of here. Help me!" Surely, I thought, Lou would take care of me.

"Betty? Are the zombies hurting you?" Lou sounded close to panic.

"Stryker shot her. She needs help," Carter called out.

"You did what?" The only other time I'd heard such anger in Lou's voice was right before he stabbed a demon with a consecrated knife. If Joseph was on the receiving end of that wrath, then it wasn't going to end well. Lou was almost always a quiet, calm guy. He had long been a logical voice of reason in The Seekers. But when Lou was truly angry, I'd learned, he was ferocious.

On second thought, Joseph was the one with the gun, and he'd already proven that he wasn't afraid to put it to use. Lou might be shot before he could ever lay a hand on Joseph.

"Lou, I'm all right," I called. "Carter and I are both fine. Don't go getting yourself shot on my account." I felt utterly betrayed by Lou, but I still cared about him too much to let him take a bullet for me. I shut my eyes again, as if I could shut out the scene happening outside the barn.

When Lou spoke again, I could tell he was trying to restrain himself. "What's the plan then, Stryker?"

"Simple. She's in there with the zombies, and if the demon wants to get her out, he's got to get past me."

I felt a light tickle of air against my ear as a quiet voice said, "Enjoying the show?"

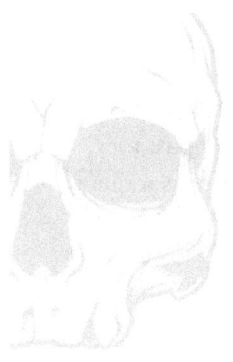

FIFTEEN

I opened my eyes and found myself face to face with Maxwell. My lips opened to cry out his name, but I stopped myself just in time. Instead, I threw my arms around his neck. "Maxwell," I breathed.

Maxwell's hands were already running down the length of my body. Instead of doing it romantically, though, I knew he was checking on my injuries. "My leg is the worst," I whispered.

When he was satisfied that I wasn't going to bleed to death anytime soon, Maxwell turned his ice blue eyes to my face. "I've missed you," he said.

"And I've missed you, but you're in danger here."

Maxwell actually smiled. "I know."

"What are we going to do?" I gripped Maxwell's hands, feeling my hope swell.

"Fight back, of course." Maxwell glanced at Carter and pointed to a far corner of the barn, then pulled me to my feet. When the three of us were there, as far out of earshot as we could be, Maxwell spoke again. "Stryker is bad news. His reputation is so bad that most priests won't even work with him. Only a handful are willing to pay him the bounty for a demon."

"Why?" Carter asked.

Maxwell gestured at my leg. "Because he'll take whatever measures are necessary. I wouldn't be surprised if some of these zombies were just ordinary people who got caught between Stryker and a demon."

I wiped at my mouth with the sleeve of my shirt. I couldn't believe I'd kissed the guy.

"Stryker wants me, but he'll kill either of you, or even Lou for that matter, if you get in the way," Maxwell continued. "The trick is to make it look like you're escaping without my help. Keep yourselves in enough danger so that Stryker will continue waiting for me to show up, instead of just shooting you."

"Will Lou help us?" I asked.

Maxwell sighed and ran his hand through his dark hair. It already stuck up in a purposefully disheveled style, so he was in little danger of messing it up. "He doesn't want you getting hurt, that's for sure. I knew he'd intervene if I told him you were being harmed."

"You made the call to him," I said.

Maxwell nodded. "A little anonymous tip. He thought I was a fellow hunter. Your friend has really gone down the self-righteous path, Betty."

"I just hope he has a better moral compass than Joseph."

"That bastard Stryker will shoot me in a heartbeat if I try anything," Carter said. "I already messed up his plans once."

"That's why you're going to go after Lou. We need to separate these three. Carter, you distract Lou. I'll tackle the woman; she'll be easy to subdue. Betty, you'll have to hold off Stryker until I can deal with the woman."

"I'd prefer it if you don't kill anyone," I said tentatively. "Believe me, part of me wants to, but if we sink to that, we're no better than them."

Maxwell raised his eyebrows. "The fat one had it

coming. He's lucky I didn't tear off each of his fingers, one at a time, before I…"

"Okay, okay," I said, raising my hands. "I don't need the visual. And yes, I'm relieved that I never have to deal with him again. Now, how exactly are we going to get out of here?"

"We need a way to get out of this barn that doesn't involve going through the door," Maxwell said. "Carter, help me look for loose boards."

It didn't take long for the two of them to find a board that could be pried away, leaving just enough room for someone to wiggle their way outside. Maxwell and Carter returned to me, and Maxwell began laying out his plan with, "Betty, can you act?"

I started crying as loudly and agonizingly as I could. Maxwell had dematerialized, leaving me alone with Carter and the revenants. Outside, I heard Joseph's quick steps as he approached the barn door.

"What's wrong?" he shouted.

"It's my leg," I answered, hoping my voice sounded weak and hopeless. "It won't stop bleeding."

"It's still bleeding? Wrap something around it."

"She needs stitches," Carter joined in. "She's lost a lot of blood."

Joseph didn't respond, and I thought he was going to ignore me. *Wouldn't be the first time*, I thought. Carter shouted, "You did this to her, Stryker. Now help her."

Still, Joseph didn't answer. The silence stretched, and I grew nervous that our plan would fail. I knew Lou must have gone elsewhere because I never heard him speak up in my defense. He was so angry that I guessed he had distanced himself from Joseph so he could cool down a little.

There was a jangling sound as Joseph opened the lock, and the barrel of his gun was the first thing I saw when he opened the door. Maybe he suspected something, or maybe he was just getting paranoid as he waited for Maxwell's anticipated rescue effort, because he waved the gun at Carter. "Get back there; I don't want you near me."

"Fine. Just take care of Betty," Carter said, his hands held up in surrender as he backed away.

Joseph peered down at me and whistled. "I didn't think I got you that bad." He didn't sound one bit apologetic about it, either.

My leg was looking worse than ever. The bleeding had actually slowed down after Carter had tied his sweatshirt around my thigh, but Maxwell wanted me to really sell my injury to Joseph. To make it look worse than it was, Maxwell had deftly sliced open his own arm and allowed his blood to soak my leg. Demons heal quickly, and by the time Maxwell's cut began to close, I had a blood-soaked leg that made me squeamish, even knowing that most of it wasn't even my own blood.

"I can bring the first aid kit here. I've got a suture kit, too," Joseph said.

I screwed up my face and gave Joseph the best pitiful expression I could muster. "Please take me back to the lodge. It's so dirty in here, and the smell is so bad."

"Fine." Joseph reached down, grabbed my upper arm, and yanked me to my feet. I shrieked with real pain as I landed on my injured leg. Carter looked at me, and I could practically hear the "good luck" thoughts coming from him. I quickly glanced around as I left the barn, and I saw no one else nearby. I gave Carter a short nod; this was his chance to get out of the barn without being heard or seen.

Joseph kept his hand clamped on my arm as he pulled

me down the trail to the lodge. I was limping more than I really needed to and keeping up a stream of groans, moans, and expletives. We passed Adrienne on the way, who stopped and stared at the odd sight we presented.

"Watch the barn. The other one is still in there," Joseph commanded.

I breathed an inward sigh of relief. Now Joseph and Adrienne, the two we were most concerned with, were going to be separated. I didn't know where Lou was, but Carter would be able to deal with him.

When we reached the lodge, Joseph headed straight for the kitchen. He threw me into a chair in one corner, somehow keeping his gun on me while searching through the drawers with his free hand. "It's not like I can run," I said.

"Shut up."

Again, I was struck with the horror that I'd actually felt something for this man. Joseph had been so charming and such a welcome respite from the loneliness I had been feeling that I'd never suspected him of being so violent. I'm usually a good judge of people, and I pride myself on being able to sense when someone isn't being straight with me, but I'd never seen it coming with Joseph. I guess I had just been too anxious to feel like someone wanted my company.

"I'm so glad I never slept with you," I said. The words were out of my mouth before I could stop them.

Joseph stopped his search and turned to me. "You would have enjoyed it."

"Would it have stopped you from shooting me?"

"No. You were always just bait for us. I tried seducing you in hopes that it would make the demon jealous and provoke him to attack. Although, if we had slept together, it would have been a nice little bonus for me."

"You're disgusting."

Joseph laughed and returned his attention to the kitchen drawer. "You didn't think so that night on the beach. Ah, here they are." He pulled a first aid kit out of the drawer, as well as a small black case.

Despite his willingness to hurt me, Joseph at least wanted me alive and conscious. I was no good to him dead, and he happily told me that calling for help or crying should spur Maxwell into action. "I'm surprised he hasn't shown up yet. I doubt he left the island after he killed Rob last night."

While he bragged about the perfection of his plan, Joseph cut open my jeans and assessed the wound. It had started bleeding again during the walk from the barn, and it stung when Joseph swabbed it with an alcohol-soaked pad.

I didn't worry too much until Joseph opened the black case and I saw the instruments inside. I tried to pull away, but there was nowhere to go. "Have you ever given stitches before?" I had survived falling, stabbing, and a shooting, and now I was getting panicky over a little needle. In reality, I was just getting panicky over everything. I was worried about Maxwell and wondered if he had taken care of Adrienne yet. I was also concerned for both Lou and Carter. I didn't want either of them getting hurt, and I hoped that Carter could deal with Lou without resorting to violence.

"I've given them to myself many times," Joseph was saying. "Being a demon hunter is a sure way to get a lot of scars."

I had to turn my head away when Joseph brought the needle down to my skin. The prick was sharp, and I sucked in my breath. It wasn't excruciating pain, but I was quickly reaching my limit for the amount of pain I could handle in one day. I kept my eyes squeezed shut and my jaw clenched while Joseph worked. When he announced that he was done, I looked down and saw a fairly neat row of stitches. At least he had done a good job.

Something bright caught my eye while Joseph put a bandage over my wound. It was an ornate piece of silver tucked into his waistband. I hadn't seen it before because the drape of Joseph's jacket had hidden it. I had no doubt that the silver was the handle of a consecrated knife, dipped in holy water and blessed by a priest.

Maxwell was in danger because of me. For that matter, Carter was in danger because of me. For the first time all day, my fear dissolved, and I felt anger take its place. I was being used so that Maxwell could be banished, and I was tired of it. I'd been waiting on Maxwell to come rescue me, but now I wanted to rescue myself. It wasn't fair to put Maxwell and Carter in danger, and it was silly to just sit around and wait for some knight in shining armor (well, a demon, at any rate) to come in and save the day.

I stood up quickly, my anger overcoming any sense of logic or caution. I inhaled deeply, ready to unleash a tirade, but instead of words, the only thing that came out of my mouth was a cry of pain. My leg protested loudly at being under my weight, and I abruptly sat back down. So much for saving the day on my own. Joseph was looking at me with a mixture of concern and humor. If I had started yelling at him, I doubt it would have done anything but cause me more pain. No, I decided, I'd have to be sneaky if I was going to get away from him.

"I'd take you back out to the barn, but I'm not sure your leg can handle it," Joseph said.

"Let's just stay here," I suggested. "Does it really matter where you have your big showdown?"

"It does. The kitchen has a back door as well as the door to the dining room. That's two points from which the demon could enter, unless he's stupid enough to materialize right in front of me."

"Silly me, I must have missed that lesson in Demon Hunting 101."

"You can laugh, but it's that kind of knowledge that has kept me alive all these years."

"And how many years is that? How many demons have you banished?"

Joseph stood proudly, and he smirked as he answered, "Six."

That didn't seem like a big number, but then again, demons running around in human form weren't all that abundant.

"So Maxwell will be your lucky number seven," I said.

"It's taken me nine years to get this far. I'll be the first modern-day hunter to reach that number."

Now it was my turn to smirk. "I heard that a lot of priests won't work with you because you use such unorthodox methods."

Joseph leaned down until his face was just inches from mine. His eyes blazed as he said, "And where did you hear that?"

Oh, no. I'd gone and opened my big mouth. I didn't have to answer Joseph's question. I'm sure he could tell just by the deer-in-the-headlights look on my face that I'd given away something important.

"When did you talk to him?" Joseph roared. I flinched as I felt his spittle spray onto my cheeks.

I thought quickly. If I confessed that Maxwell had shown up in the barn, then Joseph would know that Maxwell was on the way. Instead, I said, "He showed up in my room a couple nights ago. He told me about you then."

"I don't believe you."

"It's true. It was the night the cold front came through, and I was really cold. He materialized in my room and kept me warm."

Joseph stood again, and his nostrils flared. "He showed

up when you weren't in any danger? The whole point of all of this was to put you in danger so he'd come to your aid, and now you're telling me that he just showed up because you had a little chill? This is ridiculous! I never thought that dealing with a demon in love could be such a damn difficult thing to do."

Joseph hit the suture kit, sending it flying. "Unpredictable!" The first aid kit was next. "Unreliable!" He loomed over me then, and his hand smacked hard against my cheek, making me reel. "UNBELIEVABLE!"

I was still blinking away the spots in my vision when Joseph dragged me to my feet. I didn't have far to go: he shoved me into the walk-in pantry, pushing me to the very back so that he could squeeze in as well. He left the door open, facing the entryway like a soldier guarding his queen.

And then we heard it: the quiet pop that a demon makes when it materializes.

Maxwell had come to rescue me.

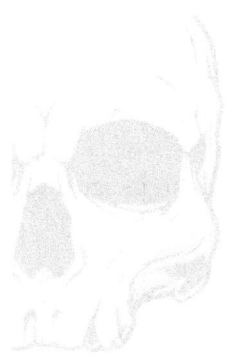

SIXTEEN

I couldn't see Maxwell, but I could hear his slow footsteps in the kitchen. I strained to peek over Joseph's shoulder and noticed that he'd drawn his knife.

Quietly, I reached up and grabbed a bottle of wine off one of the pantry shelves. As soon as I saw Maxwell appear in the doorway, I thought the bottle down hard on Joseph's skull. It made a loud thud but didn't break. Maybe that only happened in Hollywood. Still, I made Joseph stumble, and I jumped on his back, hoping to distract him.

I didn't have an actual plan, but I wrapped my arms tight around Joseph's neck and figured that, if nothing else, I would at least make it hard for him to confront Maxwell.

In fact, if I had thought over my plan at all, I probably would have acted differently. Joseph brought his knife up to my arm, holding the long blade against my skin. "What are you going to do, demon? Come any closer, and the whore gets it," Joseph said.

Whore? Well, that seemed a little overly dramatic. Apparently Joseph had very decided feelings about women who dated demons.

Maxwell instantly backed away, his hands held up. "I think you've put Betty through enough already," he said.

"Yes, and it's all been on account of you. If she dies, it will be your fault."

"I've been around for many years, Stryker, and I've learned that all too often, the hunter begins to resemble his prey. You've forsaken the very morals that led you down this path in the first place."

Joseph seemed to forget all about me in his indignation. "I most certainly have not. I still seek to rid the world of evil, as I always have."

Maxwell raised his eyes incredulously. "Yet you were willing to put an innocent woman's life at stake. You are so intent on killing me that you haven't realized that you've become evil yourself."

"She associates with you. Give me one reason why she doesn't deserve death, as well."

Joseph didn't wait for an answer. He gave a great heave and flipped me over his shoulder. He simultaneously pushed me away, and I went crashing down on top of Maxwell. Somehow, Maxwell managed to stay upright, but now I was on the floor between him and Joseph.

As Maxwell helped me up, Joseph took off at a sprint, darting out of the kitchen and into the dining room. "Stay here," Maxwell said.

"I'm coming, too." I glanced down and checked to make sure that I didn't have any new wounds with which to contend. Thankfully, I didn't. Joseph had, at least, managed to throw me without getting his knife tangled up in the altercation.

Maxwell ran after Joseph, not waiting to argue with me. I briefly wondered why he didn't just materialize wherever Joseph was going, but realized we didn't actually know where that might be. I followed slowly, limping along as fast as I could. The wine bottle, I noticed, had shattered when I dropped it before jumping on Joseph's back. How come it didn't do that when I smacked his head? It might have been more effective.

I made it into the lobby just in time to see the front

door swing shut. When I got outside, I could see Joseph running toward the boat dock. I couldn't imagine why he would try to escape over the water. Maxwell could just materialize in the boat, which left very little room for banishing or killing of any kind. It seemed like a rookie mistake on Joseph's part.

I watched as Joseph ran onto the dock, making a beeline for the boat. Not only was he making a bad move, but he was, apparently, willing to leave Adrienne behind. Some partner he was.

Maxwell was catching up to Joseph and was within arm's reach as Joseph leaped into the boat. Suddenly, Maxwell disappeared. I had a clear view of Joseph turning to the dock, his gun raised. A shot sounded, but luckily, Maxwell was no longer there.

I expected Maxwell to reappear, probably on the boat, but I didn't see him. Joseph, meanwhile, didn't even start the boat's engine. Instead, he lifted one of the seat cushions and began to pull things out of the storage compartment underneath. When he stood again, I saw that he had a bow in his hands.

Joseph hadn't gone to the boat to escape at all. He simply wanted a way to kill Maxwell that didn't involve getting up close and personal.

Except up close and personal was exactly what Joseph got. Maxwell materialized directly behind him and clamped his hands on Joseph's arms. Joseph yelped, and I knew that Maxwell was burning Joseph, just as he had done to Rob. I'd been on the receiving end of that once from another demon, and it was truly the most awful pain I'd ever felt.

Joseph struggled against Maxwell's grip, but even he couldn't stand up to the agony of an incineration. He howled loudly.

I reached the edge of the dock just as Joseph began to

fight back in earnest. He rocked backwards with all of his force, pushing Maxwell off-balance. Maxwell let go to steady himself, and Joseph turned and punched Maxwell hard in the jaw. Soon both of them were so embroiled in their fight that neither saw me approach the boat.

Joseph had thrown aside his bow, and a quiver of arrows lay on the deck of the boat. As long as he was using his fists, I wasn't worried for Maxwell's safety. Even as I thought that, though, I saw the same flash of silver that I'd seen earlier. Joseph had pulled out his knife. He raised his arm, the knife shining in the sunlight, while he punched Maxwell in the stomach with his free hand. Maxwell doubled over, and Joseph reared back before bringing the knife down in an arc toward Maxwell's back.

I shouted and leaped into the boat, crashing into Joseph's side. He fell against the side of the boat, and I clamped my arms around his chest and held on tightly. Joseph struggled to stand, trying to push me away as he did so.

Joseph was still trying to disentangle himself from me when he stumbled over the shaft of his bow. I shoved against him at the same time. This time, when we fell, we toppled right over the edge of the boat into the water.

I hit the surface upside down and immediately let go of Joseph as I tried to figure out which way was up. I held still to allow my body to float upwards rather than swimming aimlessly. I looked up and could see the sunlight glancing off the surface above me. The fall really hadn't sent me that far underwater.

My face was turned upward, about to break the surface of the water, when a hand came down over my nose and mouth. Joseph's grip was strong, and he pushed me down again. I grabbed his hand and pulled it away from me, but his strong legs clamped around my neck. He held me firmly as I tried to wiggle my way out of his grasp. I clawed at him with my nails, but even that couldn't stop Joseph from trying to drown me. His head was safely above water while my lungs were burning for air.

Joseph's body suddenly jerked upward. I knew Maxwell had grabbed him, but Joseph wasn't willing to give up on me yet. The salt water stung my eyes, but I could see that Joseph still had the silver knife in his hand. All he had to do was reach up and stab Maxwell in the heart, and Maxwell would be banished.

I used what little strength I had left to sink my teeth into Joseph's arm. His grip on the knife loosened, and I pulled it from his hand, but I was still drowning.

Maxwell, I knew, was trying to incinerate Joseph. It wasn't a fast process, though, and I would be dead long before Joseph was if I didn't make it to the surface.

I brought the knife up and sliced Joseph's leg. He jerked but didn't release me. I grit my teeth and sunk it into his thigh, hoping it would be enough. Joseph's body jerked again, and I squirmed out of his grip. It felt like the surface of the ocean was a mile away, though it was only a few feet. My head broke the surface, and I heaved in a lungful of air.

Joseph had reacted so strongly to the knife that Maxwell had lost his grip on him. Faintly, I heard a voice asking what was going on, and then Joseph pushed me under again.

This time, I didn't bother trying to work my way free. I brought the knife up as hard as I could, right into Joseph's stomach. His blood poured out into the water, and I felt more anxious to escape it than Joseph's grasp.

Another hand clamped onto me, and I looked over to see Maxwell. He had either jumped in the water or materialized there to help me. Joseph thrashed about, his arms and legs flailing, as his head slipped below the surface of the water. Maxwell pulled me away and up, and as soon as my head reached the surface, a pair of hands came down to catch me under the armpits. Carter was hauling me onto the dock.

A fit of coughing overtook me, and I lay on the dock for a few moments, oblivious to everything else. It was Lou's voice that finally made me look up. "You killed him," he said.

The betrayal and disappointment I saw on Lou's face was heartbreaking. I knew that our friendship was finally over. More than that, I suspected that I'd made an enemy. I looked down at the water, where Joseph's body floated facedown. Lou was right: I had killed Joseph.

Maxwell kneeled beside me and wrapped one arm around my shoulders. He reached out with the other to delicately pry the knife from my hand. I hadn't even realized that it was still there.

"I'm sorry," I whispered.

"You have nothing to be sorry about," Maxwell said quietly.

"I didn't mean to kill him."

"He was going to kill you." Maxwell turned his attention to Lou and raised his voice. "And I suggest you remember that detail. Betty did what she had to. Joseph would have killed her."

"She shouldn't have gone after him in the first place," Lou said bitterly. He ran a shaky hand through his long black hair, his jaw clenched.

"He was trying to kill Maxwell," I protested.

"Because Maxwell is a demon, Betty, yet you keep taking his side in everything." I felt like a child who had done something really, really wrong. The chastisement from Lou was nearly unbearable, and I would have cried if I hadn't been so exhausted.

Carter sounded angry, saying, "Do you know what he

told Rob to do to her? Do you know why that guy is dead?"

I don't think Lou wanted to know. All he cared about at the moment was how betrayed he felt. "I think it's time you and I ended our partnership," Lou said, looking at Carter. "We're leaving."

That's when I noticed Adrienne's prone body lying on the dock. I could see that she was breathing, but there was a trickle of blood on her forehead. Lou hefted her over his shoulder and climbed into the boat. Carter, Maxwell, and I all sat in silence as Lou fired up the engine and drove away.

"I can go take care of them if you like," Maxwell said.

"No," Carter and I said in unison.

"Lou was my friend for too long. I don't want anything bad to happen to him," I said.

"Plus we have to decide what to do with this body before he goes floating out to sea." Carter sounded perfectly okay with the fact that Joseph was dead.

Carter and Maxwell fished Joseph out of the water, dropping him unceremoniously on the dock. "I'll take care of him," Maxwell said. He was already crouched down next to the body, his hands on Joseph's shoulders. "Carter, get Betty inside and into some dry clothes."

Maxwell didn't have to tell me twice. Watching a demonic incineration was not pleasant, so I gladly limped my way back to the lodge.

I took a super cold, and super quick, shower to get all of the saltwater and blood off me before I pulled on a dry pair of jeans and yet another borrowed sweatshirt. Carter sure had packed a lot of clothes for this trip, but I was grateful. I still had a chill once I was finally dry and dressed, so Carter and Maxwell, who had wrapped up his task in short order, tucked me into bed and promised to bring up a hot cup of coffee.

Carter elected to make the coffee, which left me alone

with Maxwell. He sat next to me on the bed, his lean legs stretched out in front of him. I snuggled against him, and he draped his arm around my shoulders. The heat radiating off him felt divine.

"Thanks for coming to my rescue," I said.

Maxwell laughed. "You hardly needed it. All I really did was motivate you and Carter to take action. Well, and I knocked the woman on the head."

"You got Joseph away from me. Until I jumped right back into the middle of it, at least."

"It is nice having you come to my rescue every now and then." Maxwell took my hand in his and massaged it gently. "I just hate that you got hurt because of me."

"I get that they brought me here as a way to lure you," I began, "but how in the world did they expect you to find me? We're in the middle of nowhere."

"I found out where you were from Daisy, actually."

"How? I didn't even tell her exactly where I was going. I couldn't, because I didn't even know myself."

Maxwell took a deep breath and shifted against the headboard. I could tell just by his body language that I wasn't going to like what he had to say. "Daisy showed up at my doorstep, worried about you. Lou knew where you were, of course, and his part in the plan was to deliver me to the island. He went to Daisy with some story about how you were in danger because ordinary ghost hunters can't cross over zombies."

"Revenants," I interjected.

"Lou hinted that only something like a demon could handle them and suggested that she contact me. He gave her the exact location of the island. So, of course, Daisy was terribly anxious when she showed up at my house. I knew something wasn't right, because I knew that you and Carter were perfectly capable of handling the zomb— sorry, revenants—on your own."

"So you knew to be cautious when you came here."

"Yes. But when I did arrive, I didn't see anything that looked out of order. I'd heard of Joseph Stryker, of course, but I didn't know what he looked like. I stayed hidden, popping over here every now and then to observe. It wasn't until last night when the fat one regained consciousness that I found out you were dealing with Stryker. I questioned him before I killed him, and I definitely wanted him awake when I started the incineration." Maxwell's eyes lit up at the memory. He recollected for just a moment before he wrinkled his nose. "I saw you kissing Stryker."

"You're the one who broke up with me," I reminded Maxwell.

"A decision which I regret, especially since it's made absolutely no difference in how much of a target you are to hunters."

I smiled and opened my mouth to ask Maxwell if he wanted to get back together. After all, if I was going to be in danger, I might as well have him around to defend me. Before I could, though, Maxwell returned to his story.

"I came that night you got caught in the rain. I couldn't sleep, so I'd materialized here, just for something to do. You were just creeping back into the lodge, looking upset about something. I hadn't planned to let you know I was hanging around, but when I saw how cold you were in bed that night, I couldn't resist."

"And I greatly appreciate it," I assured him.

"What took you out in the rain in the middle of the night, anyway?"

I briefly relayed the story of the late-night walker and my encounter with Junior, and then a thought struck me. "Wait, you were Adrienne's ghost, weren't you? The night before you came to my room, Adrienne was visited by a ghost, but I'm guessing it was just you showing up in the wrong room."

"It wasn't me. First, I didn't come out here that night, and second, I knew exactly which room was yours."

"So that means there's still a ghost wandering the lodge." I paused and thought for a moment. "No, I bet Adrienne made the whole thing up. She was just playing a role."

At Maxwell's inquiring look, I began to tell him about Adrienne's claims and her blatant flirtation with Carter. There was a lot more for me to tell Maxwell, but Carter came into my room at that moment, carrying three cups of coffee and a carafe on a tray. I happily wrapped my fingers around the hot cup that Carter handed me and took a few sips. I waited until Carter sat down at the foot of my bed before I asked, "So, Carter, what partnership was Lou talking about?"

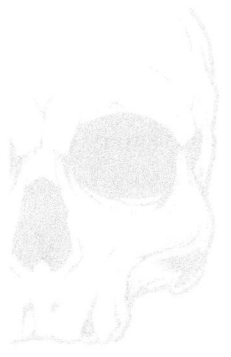

SEVENTEEN

Carter squirmed uncomfortably. With all of the excitement on the boat dock, he probably hadn't realized that I'd heard Lou telling him that their partnership was over. Carter looked down, toward the door, out the window, and down again. I never knew that Carter Lansford could be rendered speechless.

"It's a long story," Carter began.

"We're stranded on an island, so I've got nothing else to do," I said.

Carter looked apologetically at Maxwell. "Lou started taking this demon hunter stuff really seriously a couple months ago," he said. "He and I talked about it at one of the investigations we did together, but at that point, he was just reading and learning about hunting. His knowledge was something that I hoped I could tap into, and pretty soon, Lou wasn't just a walking demon encyclopedia, but a bona fide demon hunter. After he banished that demon in Atlanta, Lou got a nice paycheck from a priest in Ohio. The money and the, I don't know, thrill of the hunt really appealed to Lou. Still, demon hunting doesn't pay all that often, so hunters usually have normal jobs, too. Even Stryker did.

"I was knee-deep in negotiations for the reality show in October, and when Lou banished that demon, I realized what an asset a guy like him could be. Ghost hunting is interesting, but it's been done to death. Demon hunting, on the other hand, has a lot of potential. Think of the visuals that could create and how much fear the viewers would feel."

"Back to the story, Carter," I said.

"I'm not wrong. However, I'm also not a demon hunter. I thought that if I could get Lou on my team, we'd really have something. The trouble is, Lou can't afford to just take off from work and go shoot a show anytime he feels like it. I agreed to fund Lou's hunting in exchange for him appearing on the show."

I opened my mouth to speak, but no words came out. I was angry, hurt, and even slightly amused that Carter would do such a thing all in the name of good TV. It was so typically Carter.

Carter had been looking at everything in the room but Maxwell or me while he spoke, but now he leveled his gaze at me. "I'm so sorry, Betty. It was never supposed to be like this." With that, Carter got up and walked out of my room.

I didn't bother calling after him. I knew that anything I said right now would probably be really rude, and I'd likely regret it later. Maxwell was the first to speak. "He wouldn't have made the deal if he'd known what the result would be."

"I know," I said grudgingly.

"And at least now you know why Carter was being so nice to your whole team in October."

"Because he was trying to suck up to Lou." I smiled. "Daisy will be so relieved. She thought Carter was being nice to us because he wanted to go out with me."

"That is almost worse than you kissing Stryker," Maxwell said.

"Ick. Don't remind me." Maxwell was right, though.

Carter would never intentionally put me in serious danger. Plus, Carter had helped save Maxwell in the past. If Carter was funding Lou's hunting, then he had never intended for Lou to go after Maxwell.

I sighed and swung the covers off. I knew I wouldn't be content until I'd talked to Carter about this. "I'll be back."

Carter opened his door timidly when I knocked, as if he expected me to throw a punch. "I'm really sorry, Betty," he said again.

I pushed the door open all the way and marched inside. I did not like this cowed version of Carter Lansford and was determined to put a stop to it right away. "Yes, I'm angry," I began. Carter had followed me into the room, but at those words, he took a step backwards.

"I'm angry with Lou, though, not you," I said. "Lou once threatened Maxwell. I'm not sure what he said, but I think it boiled down to a promise that if Maxwell ever broke up with me, then Lou wouldn't hesitate to hunt him down. What makes me angry is that he was willing to use me as part of the plan."

"You heard him say that he never wanted you to get hurt."

I shook my head. "That's not the point. Lou and I used to be really close friends, and the fact that he'd lay a trap like this, using me as bait, is just wrong. He knew I wasn't over Maxwell, and I'm sure he also knew that if I was the reason Maxwell got banished, I'd be devastated."

"Well, I'm sorry for my part in it."

"Lou would have come after Maxwell, with or without you. I wish you had told me you two were teaming up, but in the end, it makes no difference. You and I are alive, and Maxwell hasn't been banished."

"We're just stuck on an island," Carter said. He smirked, and I was glad to see that he was recovering from his shame. Carter's arrogance was intolerable sometimes, but at least it was predictable.

"With two revenants that we still need to cross over," I added.

"We'll get to work on it tomorrow. I just want to know who's going to make us dinner tonight?"

"I nominate Maxwell," I said. "He's a great cook. Plus, you made the coffee, and I'm all gimpy, so I can't get around the kitchen."

"Maxwell it is," agreed Carter.

It was strange sitting down to dinner without Joseph and Rob and without Mick and Dwayne filming us. I had gone into the kitchen to offer Maxwell a hand—he declined the offer, afraid to let me anywhere near a knife after my recent luck with them—and saw that all of their equipment was still there.

"We should take it back to them," I commented over dinner.

"I think figuring out how to get ourselves, let alone anyone's stuff, off this island needs to be our first priority," Carter pointed out.

Maxwell waved his hand. "That's easy. I'll materialize back to the mainland, find a boat rental place, and come collect everyone."

"Oh, it is good to have a demon on your side," I said.

"Cheers to that," Carter said, raising his wine glass in a toast.

I felt a little better once my stomach was full, but I was still stiff and exhausted. I leaned heavily on Maxwell's arm as we walked back upstairs, my leg aching.

It was odd being in the lodge with only two other people. It felt lonely having such a big place to ourselves, and I was grateful that I had Maxwell to keep me company. He built up the fire in my room, although, thankfully, the worst of the cold front had passed, and it was much more comfortable both outside and in my room.

Maxwell took one of the oil lamps into the bathroom, and I heard the faucet in the bathtub running. I thought maybe Maxwell was going to shower, but when he came out, he extended a hand to me. "Ready for your bath?" he said.

"I am not taking a bath in that frigid water."

"No, you're going to take a bath in relaxing hot water," Maxwell said, pulling me to my feet.

I walked reluctantly into the bathroom and dipped a finger into the tub. "Ice cold."

"I've never tried this before, but I think it will work." Maxwell immersed both of his hands in the water, and his forehead creased in concentration. I watched quietly, but nothing seemed to be happening. After a few minutes, though, steam began to rise from the water.

"Maxwell, you're brilliant! And this is a lot less messy than incinerating a person." I was so caught up in what he'd just done that I forgot he had broken up with me just a month before. I put my hand to his cheek and turned his face toward me. "Thank you," I said, before pulling him close and kissing him. Maxwell returned the kiss, his lips soft and warm. Oh, how I'd missed that demonic heat that made even the most ordinary physical contact such a sensual experience.

Wait, my brain shouted, you missed it because you're not a couple anymore.

I broke off our kiss abruptly. "Sorry," I said. "I forgot."

"I can forget, too," Maxwell answered. He leaned in and kissed me again. I felt his tongue against mine as his arms slid around my waist.

"Ow!" I pulled back again, this time in pain.

"Did I bump against your leg?" Maxwell held me at arm's length, as if he was afraid that getting closer might be disastrous.

"No, it was the stab wound on my side. Well, the bad one. The other one isn't giving me much trouble."

"The other...stab wound?" Maxwell looked like he thought I might be joking.

"Rob was not delicate with me."

"If I'd known you were that injured, I would have come to your room after I took care of Rob. For that matter, I should have just gone into Stryker's room and taken care of him, too." Maxwell shook his head. "Well, regrets aren't going to get you in the tub. Are there any other injuries I should avoid?"

"There are two cuts from when I fell through the floor."

"What?" Maxwell was suddenly angry. It took me a moment to realize why.

"No, no," I said, raising my hands. "I wasn't pushed. It was a patch of rotten floor." Except, when I explained to Maxwell that I'd only fallen because a revenant had purposely been placed in a dangerous area, he didn't look any less livid.

I smiled nervously. "At least the guys behind it are both dead now, right?"

Maxwell's anger dissolved in a heartbeat. "At least you're alive now. I would say they got what they deserved, but their deaths were too easy to atone for their transgressions." His hands reached out, and he began to pull my sweatshirt off. "No sense wasting time thinking about them when I've got you right here in front of me."

Undressing me was far from sexy. I was too beat up to be alluring, and I could tell that Maxwell was concentrating harder on not hurting me than my slow progression toward naked.

Maxwell scrutinized me once my clothes were all piled on the floor. He bent over at the waist and pressed his lips against the knife wound on my left side. He repeated the action for the one on my right. Maxwell's lips were so gentle that it didn't even hurt. I sighed and put my hand against the back of his head, lacing my fingers into his black hair. He kissed the cut from my losing battle with the floor, then kneeled down and pressed his lips against the fresh bandage on my thigh. He stood then, took me by the shoulders, and slowly turned me around. I felt him kiss the cut on my shoulder blade, then his arms carefully encircled me.

I relaxed and leaned back into Maxwell. He had materialized back to Savannah earlier to put on fresh clothes, and I could feel the wool of his sweater itching against my back. I wiggled against Maxwell's chest at the sensation, and he growled softly in my ear. He pressed himself tightly against my body as his lips kissed their way down my neck to my collarbone. When he reached my shoulder, he laid his head on it and sighed. "I'm tempted to do all sorts of things to you, but I'm not sure you could take it in your state," he said.

"Sure I could. I might say 'ow' a lot, though." In truth, I'd be perfectly happy to just stand right there for the rest of the night. It felt so perfect having Maxwell close to me again.

I felt Maxwell's lips lift in a smile. "Bath first," he said.

The hot bathwater was the second-most divine thing I'd ever felt against my skin. I scrunched down until only my head was out of the water. It was awkward trying to find a way to sit that didn't put pressure on one of my injuries, but soon I was in just the right spot so that I could completely relax. I shut my eyes, and I was surprised when I felt Maxwell kissing me. He didn't stop for a long time.

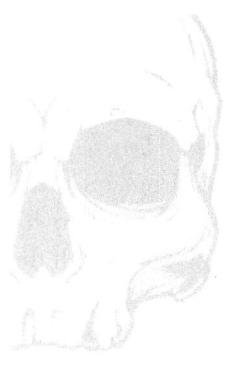

EIGHTEEN

Maxwell kissed me for so long that I actually felt myself beginning to drift off. I was more exhausted than I'd realized. I had envisioned a night of "welcome back" romance, but I knew there was no way I'd be able to stay awake for it.

While I happily soaked (and possibly dozed a little), Maxwell went to speak to Carter about setting up a watch during the night. The two of them agreed to take turns keeping an eye, and an ear, out for sounds of approaching boats.

I didn't expect Lou or Adrienne to pay us a visit, though I certainly appreciated Lou and Maxwell being so cautious. Lou, I figured, wouldn't want to face me again any time soon, and I assumed that Adrienne would realize she'd been fairly beaten when she found out that her two partners were dead. Lou had the unenviable job of telling her, and I felt sorry for him. Lou was too impressionable to get caught up in all of this without it having some lasting effect on him. In my mind, I pictured him hardening, morphing from the nice, easygoing guy I had known into a bitter man on a holy mission. I hated it, and I felt a few tears slide down my cheeks at the thought. I was really going to miss Lou, and I was really going to hate being his enemy.

Maxwell returned from Carter's room as I was thinking about Lou, and I quickly splashed some water on my face to hide the tears.

"Carter is taking the first watch. Are you done, or do you want me to reheat the water?"

I held up one wrinkled hand. "I'm turning into a prune. It's time for bed."

I wobbled when I stood and stepped out of the tub, and Maxwell had to catch me. It wasn't just time for bed; it was way past bedtime.

Maxwell didn't have any pajamas, and I jokingly asked if he planned to dash home to Savannah to fetch some sleepwear. He just stripped in answer and slid into bed beside me, just as he had a few nights before. This time, though, I was warm, happy, and, for the moment at least, safe.

I have no idea what time Carter knocked on our door to hand the watch over to Maxwell. I fell asleep just a few seconds after Maxwell kissed me and said, "Sweet dreams, Betty."

I woke up in the morning with a wonderful sense of purpose. Today, I thought, we are going to cross over Junior and Nosy. It wasn't safe for us to linger on the island, so we had no time to waste.

It took me a fair amount of time to get my limbs working properly. I was stiff and sore, and getting out of bed was a challenge. Still, I didn't let it dampen my determination. At least I was already clean and could skip the whole cold shower routine.

None of us felt up to making a big breakfast, but we found some bagels and cream cheese that suited us just fine. I really didn't care what we ate, as long as I had my morning dose of coffee. We all ate hurriedly: Carter and I were anxious to get to work, and Maxwell was eager to secure our escape by getting a boat.

We all walked outside together, but when Carter and I turned to take the trail, Maxwell stopped. "I'm off to the mainland," he said. "Be careful." He gave me a quick kiss, and his hand was still on my arm when he dematerialized.

"Who would have thought it would wind up being just you and me out here?" I said.

"Us, and Nosy and Junior," Carter reminded me.

"I was strictly talking about living people."

"So picky." Carter hefted the bag he had slung over his shoulder. We had packed both of our tape recorders, Carter's laptop, and his headphones. We hoped to speed up the crossing-over process by reviewing one EVP session while the other was being conducted.

We started with Nosy, since he had been so communicative in the past. Carter got right to the point. His first question was, "Did you know Joseph Stryker?" That was followed by a litany of questions that implied Carter thought Joseph was guilty of Nosy's death. Carter also asked Nosy if the demon who had killed him had been named Maxwell. I wasn't sure I wanted to hear the answer to that.

Now that we knew what type of questions to ask Nosy, we were able to wrap up our first EVP session with him in about fifteen minutes. I helped Carter escort Nosy back to the barn and bring Junior out to question next. Carter settled in with the tape recorder, and I found a sunny patch of grass on the other side of the clearing. I downloaded the audio to the laptop, put on the headphones, and got to work.

Like our earlier EVP session with him, Nosy proved very willing to talk about his demise at the hands of a demon. He answered the first question with a long "yesssss." Nosy followed that up by giving a hesitant no when Carter asked if Joseph was responsible for his death. So much for that theory, I thought.

There weren't any more answers, and soon I was at the last question, the one about Maxwell. I held so still while I listened for an answer that I didn't even breathe.

"Were you killed by a demon named Maxwell?" Carter's voice was loud in my ears.

I waited.

There was no response.

The session ended with a decisive click, and I felt my shoulder muscles instantly relax. I was relieved that Nosy hadn't answered in the affirmative. Maxwell had been responsible for a lot of deaths over his centuries on Earth, and I was sure that some of those victims had been hunters. Kill or be killed, as Nosy had said in an earlier session. Still, I didn't want to pin Nosy's death on Maxwell. I'd taken a strange liking to the revenant. Here was a guy who had, presumably, lived a righteous life and had been willing to face down demons. Nosy deserved peace and quiet, not this roaming afterlife.

Nosy had given us some answers, but I still didn't know why his spirit was lingering. We'd have to bring him out of the barn for yet another EVP session.

Carter finished with Junior long before I was done going over Nosy's recorded session, and I found him lying back in the grass, his hands behind his head. "You know," he began when I walked over to him, "I can see why this island was so popular with tourists. No cars, no pollution. Just trees and waves."

"I wonder what will happen to this place now that Joseph and Rob are both dead?" Carter was right; it really was a beautiful place. The lodge, I was certain, would be breathtaking if it was ever restored to its former glory.

"They'll just assign someone else to come here."

"The National Trust is going to wonder what happened to them. A couple of longtime employees who just suddenly disappear is going to raise a few eyebrows," I said.

"I'm sure it's happened before." Carter didn't sound at all worried that the sudden absence of both Joseph and Rob might mean some very awkward questions for us. After all, we had been sequestered on an island with them for a week. Surely someone would want to know if we had any information.

"I sure hope that whoever finally restores this place doesn't dig up this clearing, though," Carter added.

"You know, people are going to ask us what happened to the zombies, especially when your show airs. What are we supposed to say?"

"I hadn't thought of that. I've been so caught up in the process of crossing them over that I never considered how we'd explain what happened afterward." Carter sat up, frowning. "Damn it, I'm going to have to nix this episode, aren't I?"

"And sign Mick and Dwayne to their own non-disclosure agreements. If they could make me sign a form, then we can make them do the same to keep their mouths shut," I said.

"We came out here for nothing."

"Not nothing. We helped some very unhappy spirits get out of their bodies and into the light. I'd say that was worth the trip. Speaking of which, let's wrap this up. I want to get home to a hot shower and clothes that are actually mine."

Carter took his turn with the laptop and headphones while I had another chat with Nosy. "Do you have a message for us?" I asked. "What do you want us to know so you can be done with your time here?"

I asked everything I could think of. Carter actually

finished listening to Junior's EVP session before I got done talking to Nosy.

"Any luck?" I checked the timer on the tape recorder. It was nearly full.

"Not a thing."

Soon I was listening to my own voice asking Nosy questions. Both revenants were safely back in the barn, and Carter left for the lodge, promising to come back with some sort of lunch for us.

Nosy had remained stoically silent until I practically pleaded with him. "We're running out of time," I had said. "Please, how can we help you?"

"Sonnnnn," Nosy immediately responded. "Tellll himmmm."

Nosy was taking so long to form a sentence that I heard my own voice cut in, asking the next question. I could faintly hear Nosy's voice over my own. I replayed that section of the recording at least a dozen times, trying to make out the words. I mentally kicked myself for not waiting longer between questions.

"Tell him what?" I asked out loud as I replayed the recording yet again.

After four more attempts, the words finally took shape: "Love himmmm."

I closed my eyes in relief. "Thank you, Nosy," I mumbled. "We will gladly tell your son that you love him." Now, I thought, if we can only figure out who Nosy's son is so we can actually relay the message.

Suddenly, though, I realized that we didn't have to figure it out. Father and son had already been reunited. "Junior!" I shouted to the empty clearing. The familiarity I had felt when I saw Junior suddenly made sense. He looked like his father, even in their mutual states of decomposition.

No wonder Nosy's spirit had been unable to cross over.

If he had been killed by a demon, then it stood to reason that his son had been killed in the same confrontation. Nosy probably felt immense guilt. I doubted that they had even recognized each other when we first brought Junior to the barn. The revenants had never given any indication that they were aware of each other. It was like each soul was trapped in its own flesh-and-blood haunted house and unable to go visit the neighbors, as it were.

If Nosy was trying to send a message to his son, then Junior was probably trying to relay a similar sentiment. We could probably cross over both of their spirits within minutes.

I was suddenly very anxious for Carter to arrive so we could finish our work on Serenity Island.

I didn't have to wait very long. I was still sitting down in the grass when Carter came running down the trail. As soon as he saw me, he began to shout.

"Run, run! They're here! Go, go, go!"

I jumped up with Carter's laptop in my hands and did exactly as he instructed.

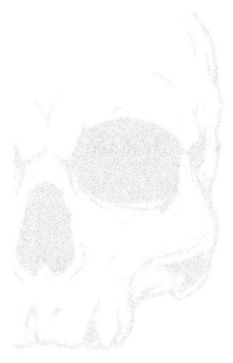

NINETEEN

I was already past the barn, heading toward the trail that led to the cabins, before I really processed what I was doing. I slowed and turned to Carter. "Wait," I said. "Who's coming?"

"Lou and Adrienne, plus more of them. Just go."

Demon hunters always have the worst timing. "But we have to cross over Nosy and Junior. It won't take long, I promise!"

"Betty, there is no time." Carter grabbed my arm and began to drag me along with him.

"No, wait, Carter, we can hide in the barn."

Carter stopped and looked at me like I had lost my mind. He considered briefly, then surprised me by nodding his head. "If I think it's a crazy place to hide, then so will they. I doubt they'll look there first."

It was ironic that we'd worked so hard to escape the barn in the first place, and now we were willingly going back inside, knowing that we'd be somewhat trapped there again.

Once we were inside, Carter found a knothole that he could use to peer outside. "No one coming this way yet," he said.

"Good, then maybe we have time." I told him about the assumption I'd made about Nosy and Junior, and

Carter looked closely at both of them. Even in the dim light within the barn, the resemblance was clear.

"How did we not see it before?" Carter asked.

"Because we weren't looking for it. Now that we know, we should be able to cross them over without too much trouble."

"Sorry," Carter said, looking out the knothole again, "but too much trouble just showed up."

Carter didn't recognize the two men walking with Lou. Adrienne and the others who had arrived must have gone down the beach to search for us. Either that, or they were combing the lodge. I wondered how long they would search for us before giving up. I didn't like the idea of playing a waiting game with demon hunters.

Maybe they would figure that we'd already left the island. It would have been the safest, and most logical, thing for us to do, and I realized that it was exactly what we should have done the night before. I had wanted to stay to cross over Nosy and Junior, but at what cost?

The three men fanned out across the clearing, but their paths were all converging on the barn. While Carter kept an eye on their progress, I looked for somewhere that we could hide. Our choices were slim: there was a hayloft that looked half-rotted, piles of old wood stacked in a corner, and a few old tarps scattered around.

The hayloft was too risky, both because of its rotting boards and because our climb up there might make too much noise. Plus, falling through another floor would definitely draw the attention of the hunters. I had no doubt that's what they were: Lou and Adrienne were looking for vengeance, and they had brought reinforcements. What would happen if they found just Carter and me? Surely Lou would never kill an innocent human, though I doubted the same was true for his companions.

Besides, I reminded myself, Lou doesn't think we're innocent anymore.

I grabbed one of the tarps. Its canvas was wet and mildewed, and it smelled toxic. I dragged it behind the pile of wood and motioned to Carter. We ducked down underneath the tarp just as we heard the lock on the door.

There was a creak, and then a male voice rang out. "Oh, the stench!" He gave a startled yelp, and I knew he'd seen the revenants. "Why didn't you warn me?"

Lou's voice mumbled a response. I hoped that would be the end of it, but the voices drew closer. Two of them were inside the barn with us.

I reached out and found Carter's hand. His grip was strong, but I could feel that he was shaking, too. I tried to make myself as small and as silent as possible.

Footsteps clunked through the barn. The two men who were searching the area were clearly making quick work of it, disgusted by both the smell and the revenants themselves. One set of boots clomped closer and began skirting the woodpile.

No, no, no, no! my mind screamed.

The boots had almost reached us when I heard Lou's voice. "Nothing here but these dead guys."

The footsteps stopped, then scuffled off in the opposite direction. Lou probably had no idea that he'd just saved Carter's and my life.

The barn door was closed and locked again, though Carter and I stayed perfectly still for at least another five minutes. I was afraid to make a sound, worried that someone was still outside, listening. When I heard a noise inside the barn, it startled me so badly that I sucked in my breath. I got a lungful of dust and mildew, and I began to cough. I covered my mouth and doubled over, trying to muffle the sounds. I had panicked over nothing more than Junior's moaning.

Once my coughing fit was over, Carter and I waited another interminable length of time in fear that the men would return. When they didn't, we slowly lifted the tarp off and stood. My thighs burned from crouching for so long.

Carter made a beeline for the knothole, but he moved quietly. He looked out, then turned to me. A thumbs-up gave me the first bit of relief since we'd hidden ourselves.

Carter and I stood close together in the middle of the barn, speaking so quietly that I couldn't understand some of his words, even though his lips were only inches from my ear.

"What now?" I asked. I sure hoped Carter had a good answer for that.

"We cross over Nosy and Junior. I have the feeling this will be our last chance to do so."

I nodded and turned, only to find myself face-to-face with Nosy. He stared at me intently, and there was a glimmer of awareness in his eyes. One of those eyes, I noticed, had begun seeping a yellow liquid. Nosy hadn't looked so alert earlier, even though we'd gotten such specific answers to our questions. He had recognized the hunter that searched the barn, I was certain. Whether that hunter had recognized Nosy—or whether he'd had anything to do with Nosy's death—I would never know.

"That," I said, pointing at Junior, "is your son. Your son is here with you right now." I kept my voice low but firm.

Nosy's head slowly swiveled to the left, and he stared at his son.

Carter retrieved one of the poles, and he ushered Junior across the barn so that father and son were standing together. If they had been alive, a casual observer would have thought they were having a conversation.

"Your father has a message for you," I said to Junior.

"He wants you to know that he loves you, and he didn't mean for you to die." Okay, so I was taking a guess on that last part, but I figured it was close enough.

Junior moaned quietly.

"Your father loves you," Carter said. "You can find him in the afterlife, if you just let yourself go."

Junior's moans grew louder as his mouth opened wide. He grew so loud that I was afraid Lou and the hunters might return to find the source of the noise. Junior stared directly at his father, and his mouth began to contort.

"I think that's a smile," Carter said.

It was hard to tell, but it did appear that the corners of Junior's mouth had lifted. Junior's moan had become a wail. It faded and transformed into several short outbursts, almost like laughing. The final "ha" was cut short when Junior abruptly slumped forward into his father's arms.

Nosy fell backwards under the weight of his son, and the two landed in a heap on the floor. Carter and I instantly reached out to help. It was instinct, and we stopped ourselves before either of us actually touched the rotting flesh. Nosy turned his head toward us, and I swear he smiled, too, before his body went limp. He had recognized his son and crossed over to be with him.

The whole scene actually left me a little teary-eyed. There is a great deal of satisfaction in ghost hunting, both in helping families who have a ghost and in helping the ghosts themselves. But to see two spirits cross over in such a physical way was especially moving.

Carter broke the silence when he reminded me that we had to be on guard. "We also," he added, "need to figure out some sort of escape plan."

"We can't get off the island until Maxwell gets back," I reminded him.

"I am back." I turned and saw Maxwell in a corner of the barn. Carter and I hadn't even noticed his arrival.

"We're in trouble," I said in greeting.

"I know. I saw the boat at the dock. I just hope no one heard or saw me approaching the island." Maxwell, who was usually really confident about, well, everything, seemed unusually worried. It was disconcerting.

Maxwell seemed to sense my feelings, because he came over and took my hand. "We'll be fine," he said quietly.

Maxwell had managed to pull his boat in next to the shipwreck. It was, he hoped, hidden enough that no one would see it without walking right past it. The hunters could search the beach all the way down to the wreck without ever seeing the boat. If they walked past the wreck, though, we were in big trouble.

"We can use my loose board to get out of here," Carter said. "The question is, when do we go for it? They might give up and leave the island, or they might camp out and wait for us."

"The longer we wait, the more chance of them finding us or the boat," Maxwell said. "We need to go now. I'll materialize out in the woods on the edge of the clearing. I can scan the area without being seen myself. Hang on."

Maxwell dematerialized without waiting for us to agree with him. He was back in under half a minute. "It's clear for now. Let's go, but be careful."

Maxwell popped back out so he could keep watch while Carter helped me squeeze through the gap left by the loose board he'd used the day before. I glanced back as I edged my way out and got one last look at Nosy and Junior. They looked sad and abandoned in their heap. I hoped that the hunters would at least have the decency to bury them. They should at least do so to cover any sign of the strange events on Serenity Island.

I sprinted across the clearing and into the woods. Maxwell was about ten feet inside the tree line, and I didn't even see him until I was under the shade of the pine trees, too. Carter followed me, and I was glad to have at least one step of our escape complete.

"We can take the trail to the cabins, then cut left and walk up the beach to the shipwreck," I said.

Maxwell gave a curt nod. "Just be ready to dive into the woods any second."

We made our way as quietly as possible through the underbrush until we stood at the edge of the trail. I was tempted to veer back into the woods; it felt a lot safer there. But as Carter had pointed out after plowing into a palmetto bush, walking in the woods was far too loud.

We walked in a single file down the trail. Maxwell led the way, materializing ahead of us every so often. He'd wait for Carter and me to catch up, then scout ahead again. Meanwhile, Carter pretty much walked backwards, his eyes and ears intent on the path behind us.

The trail took one final turn before opening out onto the beach with the remaining cabins. A few yards before that last turn, Maxwell instructed Carter and me to duck into the woods once again. Maxwell was gone a lot longer this time, and I began to worry.

I was debating venturing out to look for Maxwell when he materialized right in front of me. "Get back, quietly!" he hissed.

Carter, Maxwell, and I picked our way further off the trail and crouched down behind a mass of scrubby bushes. Hiding behind things was going to become a habit if I wasn't careful.

I began to ask Maxwell why we were hiding, but I got my answer before I could even ask. I heard the sound of quiet footsteps. One of the groups of hunters was walking from the cabins toward the barn, and they were being as clandestine as possible. I hoped that we had been just as quiet. If we had been overheard, then we'd have to make a run for it, and there was no way I could outrun men who were, I presumed, bigger and stronger than me. They probably hadn't been shot, stabbed, and half-drowned, either.

The footsteps slowly moved on down the trail until I could no longer hear them. Soon, voices sounded from the direction they had gone. Maxwell leaned close and whispered, "Half of them took the trail from one end and half came from the other end. They must know we're still on the island."

Maxwell looked at Carter and me, a finger over his lips, and disappeared. When he came back, he was smiling.

"They're all in a group, and they're heading back to the lodge," he announced. "This is our chance."

We moved quickly as soon as we got to the trail now that we didn't have to worry about how much noise we made. The cabins were soon behind us, and we walked up the beach in the direction of the shipwreck.

Maxwell materialized near the lodge again to make sure the whole group was still there. He soon came back, but this time, he wasn't smiling.

"Three of them are heading for the dock. I think they're going to take the search to the water." Without another word, Maxwell disappeared again.

With that in mind, I panicked when I heard the sound of a boat motor a minute later. I froze, my feet cemented to the sand. Carter grabbed my arm and yanked me behind a fallen palm tree.

A moment later, Carter laughed self-consciously. "It's Maxwell. He's picking us up."

I peeked out over the top of the tree trunk and saw Maxwell piloting the fanciest, sleekest speedboat I'd ever seen. He sure didn't mess around when it came to expensive modes of transportation. I had thought his sports car was nice, but this boat was a whole new level of luxury for me.

My feeling of having reached the upper class faded when I realized we would have to swim to reach the boat. I waded into the cold water as fast as I could. As the bottom of the ocean fell away beneath my feet, I began to swim awkwardly. Carter made much better progress than me and was soon in the boat with Maxwell.

I heard the sound of a second boat just as my hand grasped the small ladder hanging over the back of the boat. The hunters had caught up with us.

The dual engines next to me roared to life, and the boat began to move forward. Carter reached down and grabbed me by the arms, hauling me up the first two steps of the ladder. That got me mostly out of the water, and I scrambled over the side of the boat on my own. I sank down onto the deck while Carter hauled in the ladder. Maxwell was already maneuvering us away from the island.

Something whizzed past my line of sight. I vividly recalled the night that Maxwell and I had gone to Fort Pulaski, and a demon hunter had nearly banished him with a consecrated arrow.

I lurched to my feet and headed for Maxwell. I had to keep my hand on the railing to keep from falling over. Between the waves and the speed Maxwell was maintaining, our ride was anything but sedate.

"Arrows!" I shouted at Maxwell. The wind was loud, but I was louder. Maxwell instantly dropped down so he wouldn't be such an easy target. I chanced a glance toward the other boat and saw that they were only about fifty yards away.

"Carter, take over," Maxwell instructed. It was a good thing that Carter knew how to handle such a powerful boat. The only boat I'd ever piloted was a paddleboat in the lake behind my grandma's house. Carter took the wheel as we sped toward the inlet.

An arrow lodged in the seat cushion next to me, and I looked over at the hunters. Either the two men with bows had terrible aim (actually, considering they were shooting from one moving boat to another, they were doing quite well), or they didn't care which of us they hit. I decided to err on the side of caution and stayed flat against the deck next to Maxwell.

That left Carter vulnerable. I did the best thing I could think of: I found a life jacket and helped Carter into it while he continued to steer. Our boat was much more powerful than the one the hunters were on, and already they were falling behind. If a stray arrow did catch Carter, I hoped the life vest would keep it from doing any permanent damage.

Five minutes later, when I'd seen no more arrows flying overhead, I ventured a peek over the railing. The hunters had fallen even further behind, though they continued to pursue us.

I don't know if there are speed limit laws when it comes to boats, but if there are, then Carter probably broke them. He never eased back on the throttle as we sped up the river.

A sudden, terrible thought hit me. I stood up and edged close to Carter. "What are we going to do without your car keys?" I shouted over the wind.

Carter smiled and pulled his keys out of his pocket. "I grabbed these and my wallet when I went to the lodge to make lunch," he said. "Call it a hunch."

I could have hugged Carter for his foresight, but decided it was better to let him concentrate on steering the boat.

I rejoined Maxwell, who was sitting calmly on the deck of the boat. He didn't look nearly as worried now as he had before. I didn't try to say anything over the noise; I just took his hand and hoped that we had passed through the worst of it already.

I was instantly alert when Carter cut the throttle and the boat slowed dramatically. "What's wrong?" I asked as I jumped up. My eyes turned to the boat behind us, but they were so distant now that it would take them a while to catch up with us, even at our slow pace.

I looked forward and saw smokestacks rising over the river. We had reached the paper plant where Carter had parked his car. It felt like ages ago that he had pulled his Mercedes into that lot and we had met Joseph and Rob for the first time. I chided myself for not suspecting something from the start: there's no way I could have known, but I felt like I should have, anyway. From here on out, I thought, trust no one.

Carter glided the boat up against the dock. He cut the engine and gave Maxwell a rueful smile. "The rental place might charge you a little extra for not returning their boat."

Maxwell, already stepping gracefully onto the dock, shrugged. "Leave the key in it. They'll find it eventually." Maxwell reached down and grasped my hand, pulling me up onto the dock.

The other boat was closer now. "We need to hurry," I said.

"Let's go." Carter took off, followed closely by me. Maxwell brought up the rear, and we were in the car and pulling out of the parking lot before the hunters even reached the dock.

I gasped and hurried to buckle my seatbelt as the car careened around the turns on the narrow road. I was in the front seat next to Carter, and I shut my eyes more than a few times. If the hunters didn't kill us, then Carter's driving might.

"They don't even have a car. They can't chase us," I

pointed out after the rear end of Carter's Mercedes kicked out violently. Carter drove a little slower after that, but not much.

We all felt like we'd broken free when we were finally on the interstate heading north. Savannah was still almost an hour away, but we were back in the civilized world. We were surrounded by cars and people, and no one would be rolling down their window to shoot arrows at us.

"Carter, it was smart of you to grab your keys and wallet," I remarked. "I've lost everything. My driver's license, my credit card, my cell phone, my clothes…"

"You're still alive," Maxwell reminded me. He was sitting in the backseat, and he leaned forward to squeeze my arm. "You can replace what you lost."

I nodded. Maxwell was right. I could replace all of those things within a week. Carter's laptop was lost, too: I had left it in the barn. Still, all three of us were alive and heading home, and although I had gotten the worst of the injuries, I would be just fine once I healed.

We were quiet for a while, too tired and introspective to speak. It was Maxwell who finally began the conversation I didn't want to have. I'd been trying to convince myself that getting home meant this was all over. It didn't.

"We have to discuss what happens next," Maxwell began.

"We all live happily ever after?" I said hopefully.

"This isn't the end. I think the hunters will lay low for a while to regroup, but they will come back. Betty, you killed one of their own. Carter, as far as Lou is concerned, you've chosen your side. Both of you are going to be just as much a target as me."

Maxwell's next sentence was chilling. "The demon hunters have declared war on us."

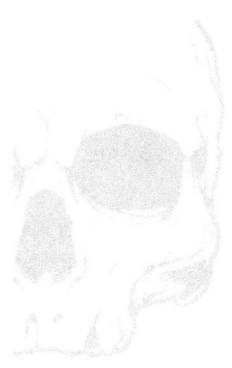

TWENTY

As Interstate 16 gave way to the quiet streets of Savannah, I felt a flood of relief. It was late afternoon, and the sun was gleaming off the gold dome of City Hall. I was home. At the moment, I didn't care that a horde of demon hunters might have me in their sights. Maxwell had said we shouldn't have anything to worry about just yet, and I heartily agreed.

Carter pulled into the narrow lane behind my apartment, and it was everything I could do not to sprint to my front door. Instead, I turned to Carter, who had alighted with us.

"I'm sorry again about all of this, Betty," he said. "It just all went to hell, didn't it? The show, our lives, my wardrobe."

"Show?" Maxwell interjected.

"I'll explain later," I said. "Carter, you couldn't have known that any of this was going to happen. Those guys gave us no reason to distrust them."

"Call me if you hear anything. We need to be prepared." Carter's face was grim.

"Same here. Even if you just feel like something weird is going on, let one of us know. A hunter trying to reach Maxwell started following me a while back. They may not attack us in broad daylight, but you can bet they'll be keeping tabs on us."

Carter nodded and began to climb back in his car.

"Wait," I said. "You can at least give me a hug. After all, we nearly died together."

Carter wrapped his arms around me and squeezed tightly, but he just as quickly stepped back. "You smell like zombies," he said.

"Gee, thanks."

Carter leaned toward me and sniffed the air gingerly. "It's your hair. Something from that tarp we hid under must have stuck to your hair."

I bent forward at the waist so I could rub the top of my head against Carter's shirt. "There," I said, "now you can take some home with you."

"You're disgusting."

And here I had just begun to think that Carter was human, after all. If nearly getting killed at the hands of a rogue demon hunter didn't cure him, then nothing would. I just smiled. "Bye, Carter. Call me when your tell-all book about this comes out."

Carter's eyes lit up as he considered the idea. I could tell that his mind was already writing the outline as he drove away.

"Let's get you inside," Maxwell said.

"Let me get my keys out," I said. It was followed closely by, "Oh, damn it, I don't have my house key!"

"I can help there. Go to the front door, and I'll let you in." With a quiet pop, Maxwell disappeared. He soon opened the front door wide for me, and I was finally home.

It almost surprised me that nothing had changed. Over the past...how long had it been?

I asked Maxwell just that.

"Today is Saturday," he told me.

I had been gone for a week and one day. In that time,

I'd been shot, I'd been stabbed twice, I'd fallen through a hole, I'd killed someone, and I'd been chased by demon hunters. I'd also reconnected with Maxwell, helped a bunch of revenants, and almost had a supporting role on a reality show.

A little mew brought me out of my reverie. Mina trotted over to me, and I happily scooped her up. I squeezed her against my chest and felt her purring. "Mina, you would not believe the adventure I had," I told her.

I sat down on the couch, Mina in my lap, and Maxwell joined me. He took my hand and kissed my fingers.

"I guess it really isn't safe to date you," I said sadly.

Maxwell laughed. "No, it's not, but clearly you're not safe without me, either." His expression quickly sobered as he said, "I'm sorry, Betty. I really thought you'd be safe if I broke up with you. I guess the hunters knew that I still loved you, even if we weren't together. I had been following you to make sure you were safe from any demons who might want to avenge Tage's banishment. Instead, all I did was put you in more danger."

"I survived, at least," I said.

"You were amazing." Maxwell leaned in and kissed me. "And even after everything you went through, even knowing that there were hunters searching for you, you still made sure those spirits were put to rest. That's the kind of selfless sacrifice that makes the difference between a demon and a human."

I smiled and nuzzled against Maxwell's shoulder. "You rescued Carter. Doesn't that count as a selfless sacrifice?"

"No. He helped take care of you, and whether or not you want to admit it, you two have clearly become friends. If he's important to you, then he's important to me."

"We're going to have to all work together to fend off these hunters, aren't we?" I asked.

"Yes. We all need to be vigilant, and I want you to start learning fighting techniques."

I groaned.

"It's not that bad," Maxwell assured me. "Whenever you show improvement, I promise to reward you well."

"I've got a whole week of vacation left. That gives us plenty of time for some intensive training." I raised my head and cocked an eyebrow. "And intensive rewarding."

Maxwell just kissed me in answer.

"I missed you," I said when he broke our kiss to pull me to my feet.

"And I missed you terribly. You'll be getting more than enough of me now, though."

"What do you mean?"

"I'm not letting you out of my sight. Either I'm sleeping over here, or you're sleeping at my house. It's too dangerous for either of us to be sleeping alone, especially since Lou knows where we both live. As of right now, you and I are living together." Maxwell paused. "But I don't think we should tell anyone. The less the hunters can find out about what we're doing, the better."

"Oh. How…romantic." I wasn't even sure that I wanted Maxwell around constantly. We hadn't dated long enough to make it to that stage. His hands sliding up under my sweatshirt to lift it over my head made me think twice. Maybe it would be nice to have Maxwell around all the time.

My bra was next. Yes, I could definitely enjoy our new living situation.

Maxwell continued to undress me all the way to the shower. At least I would have some help getting the zombie smell out of my hair.

A NOTE FROM THE AUTHOR

Thank you for reading *Ghost of a Memory*! Before you dive into *Ghost of a Hope* to find out how it all ends, will you please take the time to leave a review? By reviewing a book, you help both the author and other readers.

I'm grateful for your support!

Beth

ACKNOWLEDGMENTS

As always, thanks to Mom for her sharp eyes and to my husband Ed for his willingness to be a test reader.

NEXT IN THE SERIES

GHOST OF A HOPE

BETTY BOO, GHOST HUNTER BOOK FOUR

THE DEMON HUNTERS HAVE DECLARED WAR IN SAVANNAH.

Two weeks after her return from Serenity Island, Betty "Boo" Boorman is expecting retribution from the demon hunters at any moment. They have remained quiet so far, but the ghosts of Savannah, Georgia, have not.

A series of violent hauntings all have similarities to past cases The Seekers have investigated, putting Betty and her team in danger. A surprise demon attack makes Betty realize she has more to fear than vengeful hunters and vicious ghosts.

When the demon hunters finally make their move, the lives of Betty, Maxwell, Carter and The Seekers will be irrevocably altered.

BOOKS BY BETH DOLGNER

The Betty Boo, Ghost Hunter Series
Paranormal Romance

Ghost of a Threat

Ghost of a Whisper

Ghost of a Memory

Ghost of a Hope

The Eternal Rest Bed and Breakfast Series
Paranormal Cozy Mystery

Sweet Dreams

Late Checkout

Picture Perfect

Scenic Views

Breakfast Included

Groups Welcome

Quiet Nights

The Nightmare, Arizona Series
Paranormal Cozy Mystery

Homicide at the Haunted House

Drowning at the Diner

Slaying at the Saloon

Murder at the Motel

Poisoning at the Party

Clawing at the Corral

Manifest

Young Adult Steampunk

A Talent for Death

Young Adult Urban Fantasy

Nonfiction

Georgia Spirits and Specters

Everyday Voodoo

ABOUT THE AUTHOR

Beth Dolgner writes paranormal fiction and nonfiction. Her interest in things that go bump in the night really took off on a trip to Savannah, Georgia, so it's fitting that her first series—Betty Boo, Ghost Hunter—takes place in that spooky city. Beth also writes paranormal nonfiction, including her first book, *Georgia Spirits and Specters*, which is a collection of Georgia ghost stories.

Beth and her husband, Ed, live in Tucson, Arizona. Their Victorian bungalow is possibly haunted, but it's not nearly as exciting as the ghostly activity at Eternal Rest Bed and Breakfast.

Beth also enjoys giving presentations on Victorian death and mourning traditions as well as Victorian Spiritualism. She has been a volunteer at an historic cemetery, a ghost tour guide, and a paranormal investigator. Beth likes to think of it all as research for her books.

Keep up with Beth and sign up for her newsletter at
BethDolgner.com

Made in the USA
Monee, IL
21 September 2025

26223201R00125